Searching For Katherine

- A Novel -

by Melissa Holden

First published October 2014

Printed by Create Space

Cover art by Deborah Bretherton

Copyright © Melissa Holden 2014

The moral right of the author has been asserted.

All rights reserved. No part of this publication may be reproduced, stored in a retrieval system, or transmitted in any form or by any means without the written permission of the author, nor be otherwise circulated in any form of binding or cover other than that in which it is published and without a similar condition being imposed on the subsequent purchaser.

ISBN: 978-1502777638

For the ones who were there when I needed them

Prologue

"Hi J-Jennifer" stuttered the little boy, straightening his school tie and twisting his foot on the playground floor.

"Get out of the way little boy! You're standing on my shadow!" The little girl screeched and stepped backwards.

"Oh, I'm sorry. What's wrong with your shadow?" He stared straight into her eyes even though she was yelling at him.

"Well now it's got the cooties because you'd stood on it! Silly! Honestly - don't you know that little boys has cooties?"

"No! What are they?" he asked, sniffing and trying to hold back his tears. He didn't like being shouted at by grown ups, but especially by pretty girls.

"They're like a disease that you can give people and they last forever and ever. Now my shadows got them because you got in the way - stupid!" Little Jennifer pushed the boy out of her way and ran crying to a gaggle of girls on the other side of the playground. She pointed and laughed at him as he moped over to a vacant bench. He stayed there until his mother came to pick him up. She saw him sitting alone with a book on his lap and his glasses half way down his face and sat next to him.

"What's the matter darling? The teacher called and said you were upset today." She ruffled her son's spiky hair and kissed the top of his head. "Do you want to tell me what happened?"

"I tried to talk to the pretty girl again today." He didn't look up.

"Oh? And how did it go?"

"She yelled at me and said I gave her a disease."

"I'm sorry honey."

"Why?"

"Because she upset you."

"No she didn't - she yelled at me!" The boy stared at his mother's confused face and smiled. "She's never yelled at me before." He hopped off the bench and took his mother's gentle hand. "Let's go home for dinner now. Can we have spaghetti to celebrate?"

Chapter One

Jennifer walked out of the flat, put her iPod on shuffle and started the walk to town. Music from her time at university played into her ears, making her reminisce about her care-free three years studying her degree and socialising, she smiled as the song switched to a club anthem from her final year and brought back memories of her and her best friends going swimming in the sea at three am. She missed undergraduate life, although not enough to want to go back to university. She had a degree in Media Communications and was proud of it, but it was slowly being forgotten and taken over by her job in a book store.

It was a pleasant, if cloudy, spring day, but it wasn't warm enough to go without a coat. She pulled the itchy wool material away from her skin. Her mother had bought her the coat as a Christmas present in a hope that Jennifer would wear it. The coat was a dark blue, almost navy, with six white buttons down the front. It looked like an oversized blazer but it had got her through four months of snow, rain and plummeting temperatures - which were all blamed on climate change but she just associated the bad weather with the winter. Now all Jennifer could think about was shoving the coat into the back of the wardrobe and ignoring it for the rest of the year. The sun warmed her skin as Jennifer walked along the high street, observing the people around her: a toddler attempting to escape his pushchair; an old woman feeding pigeons; a community support officer scolding youths in hooded jumpers.

She looked at her watch, forty minutes to spare and Katherine was going to meet her for a coffee. She walked across the high street and entered the double doors of the coffee shop. There was no queue, so she approached the barista with a smile and said, "Can I have a large tea, please." She removed her purse from her bag and pulled out the coins she needed.

"Yes, of course. That's £2.95." Jennifer handed over the money and watched as the barista put the change in the till and wandered off to make her drink; chewing gum as she called out to her colleague about a 'fit guy walking in, and how it was her turn to 'have a go'. Jennifer gazed at the paper coffee cups as she waited. *Of all the drinks they sell, she must think my order is so dull. Then again, it's probably a lot easier to make. I mean, I add the milk and the sugar, all she does is put a tea bag in hot water,* she thought, fiddling with the zip on her purse. The barista returned - still chewing her gum -, handed Jennifer her drink and walked off to serve another customer. Jennifer looked around for a table and found the only one free was in the corner. She hurried over and put her drink down on the table. She sat down and pulled a book from her bag: *Discussing Wittgenstein.* She had been there for five minutes when she was interrupted by a figure hovering over her.

"Sorry, do you mind if I sit here? There's nowhere else." A tall man with tanned skin and dark hair stood in front of her.

"Oh, of course, go ahead." She pulled her tea closer to her side of the table and returned her gaze to the book. A moment later, she peered over the top of it to find him trying to read the blurb on the back, his head tilted a little to make up for the odd angle at which Jennifer held her book. She had often been told she positioned books weirdly, especially when she was sitting in a chair reading them. Katherine had frequently told her that she looked as if she were about to curl up or topple over the way she twisted herself. Jennifer paid no attention to her friend and carried on reading at strangle angles, but the strange man was now making her acutely aware of how odd she looked half-leaning, her book on a forty-five degree angle compared to the level table. She straightened up, tucking a loose hair behind her ear and tried to brush off the deep embarrassment she was experiencing as the man corrected his tilted head and apologised.

"Sorry, it just seemed interesting." He laughed, picking up his coffee cup. He was beautiful: green eyes, a killer smile and lightly tanned skin.

"It is an amazing story – it's all true." She replied.

"Really? Have you read it before then?" He asked.

"Yes. Only once though – it is a beautiful read, but I can't read the ending in public."

"Oh and why is that?" The pretty stranger enquired, his eyes looking past the book and Jennifer felt nervous, as if she were being recorded or studied by odd people in lab coats. She expected someone to show up to take her pulse or a blood sample at any moment.

"It makes me cry," she stated, still attempting to read, and yet looking at the man's face. "Have you just been on holiday?" Her subconscious question escaped from her lips, noticing the warm hue to his complexion.

He laughed and answered, "Yes I have – Bora Bora."

"My room-mate is going there in a few weeks with her boyfriend. Is it nice?"

He murmured in response as he drank his tea. He put the cup on the table and held his hand out, "I'm Marcus."

She gave him a big smile, put down her book and shook his hand. "Jennifer." She laughed, "I didn't think people shook hands anymore?"

"I'm a businessman - it's polite. And it's an excuse for some skin-to-skin contact I suppose." Marcus winked at her and she could do nothing but giggle and blush. "Well, it was lovely to meet you, Jennifer. But I have to go and take care of some business. I'll see you around?"

"Yeah, sure. I come here quite a lot so... yes." She held back a girlish squeal and straightened her back, which pushed her chest forward.

Marcus stood up, nodded goodbye and walked away from their table. Jennifer tried to return to her book, but she couldn't get his face out of her head. A few minutes later, Katherine arrived, waved at her and sat down. Her hair was messed by the spring breeze and she wrapped her scarlet coat around her frame.

"What happened?" Katherine smirked, stealing a swig of Jennifer's drink before yelling to order her own. "A tea to go please? Thanks!"

"What?" Jennifer sipped from her cup, smiling slightly.

"You're grinning like a fool!" she turned in her chair, the very same chair that Marcus had just vacated. "Did you meet a boy? Did you?" She teased.

"How did you know?" She smiled again and sighed, her tense body relaxing a little.

"Because you've got that stupid dazed on your face. You learned that grin from me you know!" Katherine winked at her friend and then ran off to collect and pay for her drink. When she came back she unravelled the scarf from around her neck and hung it over the back of her chair. Jennifer was still grinning at her cup, so Katherine waved her pink hand in front of her face to catch her attention.

"Sorry!" Jennifer laughed, "Do I look as silly as you did when you first met Joe?"

"Even worse!" The women laughed together and Katherine leaned closer. "I've got something to tell you by the way." she wriggled forward so she was in touching distance of her flat-mate.

"Ooh gossip, spill!" Jennifer winked at her best friend.

Katherine took a deep breath, bit her lip and then blurted out the words:"I'm getting married!"

"Joe proposed? Oh my - congratulations!" Jennifer squealed and grabbed her friend's hands with excitement.

"Well... Not exactly... I think he's going to propose because he's being super nice with this holiday and everything, and we've been together for nearly three years now. It just feels like it, you know?" Katherine sighed again, letting go of Jennifer's hands and leaning back in her chair.

"I'm sure he will, honey! Just you wait - you'll be on a sandy beach in Bora Bora and he'll get down on one knee in front of everyone. It'll be so romantic!" Jennifer beamed at her friend, thinking how good it was to see her happy again. Then she breathed an internal sigh of relief because it meant that Joe was sticking to the plan, even if Katherine had figured it out - she was still going to get engaged on a hot beach in the middle of nowhere. "How will you afford a wedding though, I mean no offence - but you can barely pay the rent."

"Joe has started working for some huge corporation in London, and he seems to think that it's a step in the right direction for his own business. Remember, he said the other day that he wants to run his own company and stuff? Well even if he doesn't get there, he has enough skill to work his way up in his new job. It pays pretty well too!" Katherine fiddled with her coat belt and picked at a loose thread.

"Well, I guess I should go dress shopping then!" Jennifer looked at her watch and downed the rest of her drink. "I've got to go, Kat - we've got an early delivery at work and no one but me can authorise it."

"You and that bookshop - it'll be the death of you! Maybe you should come on holiday with us?"

"And interrupt your engagement, no thank you! Besides, if I go with you I might never see that cute guy again!" She poked out her tongue and laughed as she stood up from her chair. "I'll see you after work?" Katherine nodded in response and Jennifer headed to work.

Chapter Two

Katherine and Jennifer pottered around their two-bedroomed flat their bare feet shuffling across the fluffy red carpets, waiting for an acceptable time to start getting ready. Katherine walked around with a cup of tea in one hand and a biscuit in the other, munching on the latter as she waited for her toe-nails to dry. She had used a UV nail varnish that glowed in the dark. Jennifer sat drinking berry tea underneath a blanket, watching QI on the flat screen TV they had bought a few months ago in a sale. They had picked it because it was big enough that they didn't have to squint to see it, but small enough that it didn't become the focal point of their living room - especially as they barely used it.

"Kat, do we have to go out tonight?" Jennifer whined, taking a sip from her mug. "We could have a nice early night and watch a movie or something?"

"You're so old-before-your-time sometimes, do you know that? And yes: we do have to go out tonight." She didn't look at Jennifer; she just carried on walking around with a grin on her newly-moisturised face.

She sulked for a moment before saying, "Walking won't help them dry, you know." Jennifer laughed as Katherine gave up and sat down beside her in a huff, stealing part of Jennifer's blanket with her feet poked out of the edge as so not to ruining them.

"I know, I just didn't want to sit still – tonight is supposed to be really fun! It's UV night."

"Isn't it always?" She looked at Katherine sideways, stealing her friend's biscuit and taking a bite.

"Yes, but this is UV paint." Katherine said, with mock importance, frowning at her stolen snack in Jennifer's hand. "That was mine!" She huffed.

"So, basically we are getting all dressed up to go out, but we could just stay in and paint each other with those test samples we have left over from when we repainted the kitchen," she grinned.

"They aren't glow-in-the-dark though, are they?" Katherine laughed and then drained the rest of the tea from her mug. "Do you want another cup?" she asked, picking up the two empty mugs from the coffee table.

"Yeah, go on." Jennifer wiggled back into the sofa and started flicking through the channels and not really paying attention. She was the type of person that could spend hours watching TV or scrolling through the internet, but she never really took notice of anything on a screen. She would much rather waste her time reading the books in her shop than watch TV. Her personal collection of books was large, and sat in their living room on three long shelves. They were all different colours and sizes, from different genres and years. She barely ever read the same book twice, and she never kept books she didn't like. Jennifer glanced at the books for a moment and considered reading one, but she remembered how annoyed Katherine would get when they were having a conversation and Jennifer suddenly picked up a book. Katherine said it was rude and that she was shutting people out instead of talking about things. Jennifer usually just shrugged in reply and gave in but today she wondered why she never answered her best friend's question. She was about to get up and actually choose a book when Katherine returned with a hot cup of tea for her. They sat and stared blankly at the screen, occasionally discussing something on the television and then returning to their comfortable silence.

****

"Jen?" Katherine whined from her bedroom door.

Jennifer emerged from the bathroom in a worn purple towel around her body and a green toothbrush in her mouth. "What?" she murmured.

"Which one: yellow or red?" Katherine held up a bright yellow mini dress in her left hand and a red peplum dress in her right.

"They're both awful. Where are we going?" She continued brushing, smirking underneath the white smear of toothpastes on her lips.

"That club on the high street." Katherine bit her lips and considered both dresses.

"The one with the skinny bouncer?" Jennifer asked.

"Yep."

"But why are we going out in the first place?" she whined.

"To celebrate my engagement of course - you know, because you won't be with us when it happens." Katherine looked at the dresses while she spoke.

"If it happens" she mumbled. Jennifer walked back into the bathroom and spat the toothpaste from her mouth. "Yellow," she called.

"Yellow? Are you sure?" Katherine questioned as she turned the dress to face her.

Jennifer stood back in the hallway and looked at her. "Hold the yellow one against you."

Katherine did as she was asked. "Yes, definitely yellow - the red ones too...well: red." Jennifer walked down the hall to her room and shut the door.

Chapter Three

Jennifer pushed past the sweaty, blurred bodies in the club and headed for the bar. The noise and confusion threw her off, and the queue at the main bar irritated her. She gave up and went over to the second lounge bar, hoping they would have a decent top shelf.

"Two tequilas, please - no salt or lemon," she shouted over the thudding bass track and handed over the money. The dancers feet stuck to the floor and people spilt their drinks all over the place. She made her way back to where she had left Katherine dancing, but couldn't see her. She turned on the spot, searching for Katherine in the dark neon world of the club: Katherine wasn't there. Jennifer rushed through the crowd, checking the smoking area – holding her breath against the fumes. She nudged her way back through the club to the women's toilets, yelling for Katherine but she wasn't there either.

Jennifer approached the bulky security guard and tapped him on the elbow, which was the only part of his arm she could reach without tiptoeing. "Have you seen a girl in a yellow mini dress?"

He shook his head.

She put the drinks down onto an empty table and left the club, looking outside for Katherine. She went up to the slim bouncer that the club was so famous for, "Have you seen a girl in a yellow mini dress? She's about my height, skinny and a little bit drunk?" Jennifer pushed the hair from her face.

"No, sorry - she might be inside." He responded, indifferent, watching the crowd.

"No, I've checked, I can't find her anywhere. She's my flatmate – this isn't like her just to wander off."

"She might have gone home, Miss. Why don't you call her?" He turned to another bouncer and struck up a conversation.

Jennifer pulled her phone from the black mini bag that hung from her exposed shoulder and called Katherine's phone.

"You have reached the answer phone of –" Jennifer hung up the phone and walked to the taxi rank down the street. She stopped beside the passenger door of the first taxi and motioned for the driver to unwind the window. The window sank down into the door and she leaned through slightly.

"Have you seen a girl in a yellow dress?" she asked, returning her phone to her clutch bag.

"No, sorry love - maybe she got lucky?" He grinned at her, his face half-hidden in the dark. The only light on his face beamed out from the club, the bass track still audible.

"I doubt that." Jennifer got into the back of the taxi and told him her address. She spent the drive texting and calling Katherine in a panic. When she got home, she paid the taxi driver and rushed up to her flat. Katherine wasn't there.

"Fuck." Exasperated, she called Joe. "Joe? Is Kat with you?"

"It's 1a.m, Jen!" Jennifer paced up and down the living room. She could hear the sleep in his voice.

"Yes I know, but is Katherine with you?" She kicked off her shoes.

"No. I thought you went clubbing?" Joe's voice wobbled with worry.

"Yeah, we did, but then she disappeared and no one's seen her."

"Have you checked the flat?" His tone grew higher.

"Yeah, I'm here now – Katherine hasn't been here. The front door was still locked and she isn't in her room."

"OK, I'll call some people. I'll be round in twenty." Joe hung up the phone.

Jennifer sunk into the armchair and put her head in her hands. "Where are you, Kat?"

Chapter Four

The room was dark and the bare wooden floorboards splintered her naked legs. She could feel a concrete wall behind her, but it felt rough as if the plaster was breaking off. She closed her eyes, her head pounding and she could feel the warm trickle of blood running down her face and onto her lips. The music from the club was still ringing in her ears, like a painful memory that she hoped she could wake up from. Her body felt bruised and twisted out of place but she didn't want to open her eyes and face what had happened.

Her thoughts wandered back a few hours, to her night out with Jennifer and then she remembered what had happened, in pieces as though it was one of those dramatic movie trailers from Hollywood. Someone had grabbed her arm, mumbled something and then pulled her out of the crowded club and through a black side door. She could barely see from the effects of the alcohol and the tears streaming down her face. She stumbled over her black heels as he dragged her down an alleyway and into a car. She fell to the ground and ripped her dress and the skin of her knees. The arm dragged her back onto her feet and shoved her into the back of the car. It was blue, maybe black, she couldn't tell. People around her were screaming and laughing, and the music from the club was still thudding in the background and ringing in her ears. The memory made her shudder and weep even more.

"Shut up. I told you to stop crying!" A man's deep voice echoed around her head. There was panic in his tone, but not enough for her to doubt his authority over the situation. She kept her eyes screwed shut and tried to move her hands to her face, but a rope restrained her wrists.

"Who are you?" she sobbed, "Where am I? Why are you doing this to me?", tugging at the rope in the slight chance that it hadn't been tightened enough, but as she did so the plaited fabric's grip only grew tighter still.

"Actually, I have a question first." his blurry figure moved in front of her and he put his cold hand on her ankle. She wondered where her high heels had gone, but she couldn't recall taking them off.

"What? What do you want from me?" her voice went horse as she screamed at him.

"Who are you?" His tone was harsh and cold, he snapped the question at her.

"You mean you kidnapped someone you don't even know?" She drew her legs up to her chest, she could feel the material of her yellow dress keeping her warm in the cold dawn light.

"I was aiming for someone else... What is your name anyway?" He spat his words at her, like a cobra threatening it's prey.

"Katherine, my name is Katherine." she choked.

"Hello Katherine. I'm sorry about this, really I am." For a moment Katherine thought he might actually be sorry and it was all some horrible mistake. But then she remembered that he could see her face so he knew she wasn't who he was after, but he was keeping her prisoner anyway.

"If you're sorry then let me go - I won't tell anyone, I promise. Please just let me go home to my friends." She pleaded to the man who held her life in his hands.

"I can't. You'll tell someone and I just can't have that. I'm sorry."

"Please, just tell me why. Why did you take me? Where am I? What are you going to do?" On the outside, she was calming down but on the inside she was screaming and praying for a way to escape and stop the crazy lunatic in front of her.

"Enough. Stop asking me questions!" He bent down and his hand made harsh contact with Katherine's tear-stained face and she felt her brain rattle in her head. "Shut up! Stop asking me questions and be quiet!"

"Never! You'll have to kill me if you want me to stop asking!" She flailed her legs around hoping to knock him down, but with her eyes half closed and her sight blurry, she saw his shape as if it were a shadow: untouchable and unbreakable. The man simply stepped back three feet and laughed at her. When she stopped, he crouched in front of her, stroked the face he had just moment's ago slapped and then smiled at her. Through her tears his lips looked crooked and distorted but she knew it was just fear getting the better of her. The man's hand slid down to her throat and he wrapped his right hand around it. He squeezed gently and watched Katherine struggle against him. She coughed and mutely yelled as his grip tightened, halting the air in her lungs and making the world spin.

"Do you want to breathe again?" He whispered at her, and she nodded weakly. "Okay then. Stop asking me questions and you can live, deal?" Katherine nodded once more and he let go. She gulped for air and slumped back against the wall behind her. The concrete was a cold welcome to the pain she was feeling. He stood up and backed away from her, as if he were scared of what she might do. But there was no need and as many threats on her life, Katherine knew this man would never kill her - on purpose at least. She was his prisoner and his bargaining chip.

"Are you going to use me for something? Is that your plan?" Instead of answering her questions or shouting, he just smiled and walked towards a rotting wooden door. It's orange paint had peeled away years ago, leaving just a trace of it's once bright colour. The handle was small and made of a black metal. Her vision slowly crept back into her eyes and her cell became clearer. But there wasn't much to look at: the only furniture in the room was a small bed in the opposite corner and an dark-stained oak rocking chair. Katherine assumed the bed is where she would sleep and the chair was for the man to watch her from. By the time she focused on him again, he was already half way out the door, letting the bright indoor lighting flood into the room. She titled her head, in hope she might be able to get a grasp on what kind of building she was in, or even where she was, but all she could see was the light blinding her and another door on the opposite side. It looked like a front door but she couldn't quite tell. The lack of windows around it lead her to believe she might be in a flat of some kind, so she gave up her momentary thought of jumping out of the window above her head.

The figure left the room quietly and let her cry, he gave up trying to halt her tears. She sobbed and whined and screamed until the sun was high in the sky, but no matter how bright its light got it still didn't heat her skin and stop the chill in her body that she knew was the touch of death's gentle hands. Her hope of escaping had dwindled in those precious few hours and Katherine came to peace - a stop in her destiny -, knowing that those moulding four walls, the bed and the rocking chair were the only sight she would ever see again. The light from the door was only light, and it was not her chance at salvation. She knew she was going to die in that cold, rotting room and never see her loved ones again.

Chapter Five

Jennifer lay in her bed thinking of the last time she saw Katherine – a wide smile on her face, enjoying their night out. *She didn't look depressed or sad; she didn't even look lonely when she was by herself in the club. So where is she? She's not dead... I would know. She wouldn't run away – she doesn't have anything to run from. She and Joe are going so well, I am sure he's going to propose any day now. I just wish we knew where you were so he could do it...* Jennifer looked around her bedroom: clothes on the floor, her wardrobe open. She was quite a tidy person usually, but this had thrown her. She didn't care what her room looked like – she just wanted to know what was going on. *Katherine would have told me to relax – she'd tell me to tidy something and calm down. No, I know what she would do: make me a cup of tea.*

Jennifer pulled the smothering duvet covers off her body and got out of bed. She sat perched on the edge of her bed, with her head in her hands. Her dress from the club still lay on the floor by her feet. She picked it up and held it in her hands and buried her face in it. "Where are you, Kat?" she mumbled into the dress, it's cold material shocked her as it touched her skin.

A soft knock on her bedroom door surprised her; she put the dress on the bed, got up and opened the white varnished door. Jennifer made a mental note to clean the apartment for Katherine's inevitable return. She wouldn't appreciate a messy home after such an ordeal.

"Oh, are you alright?" she asked, a little surprised to see Joe. "I thought you had gone home." Jennifer watched him standing there, a pale shadow in the dark, with not even the moon to light his face. She felt so bad for him, she might be missing her best friend, by Joe was missing his soul mate. They were inseparable. It was one of those relationships where you knew they were going to be together forever.

They were the modern day fairy tale. So why did it have to go so badly when it was just about to go so right? Jennifer didn't have a clue, but she knew Joe was suffering no matter what the reason.

Joe ran his fingers through his hair, holding his arms above his head as if he were stretching. Jennifer could see that his eyes were red, clearly from where he had been crying. The dry red skin framed his eyes and they looked like car headlights just before the story-book crash where the main characters die. Jennifer didn't like the idea of a car-crash ending for Joe and Katherine, so she removed the thought from the fore-front of her mind.

"No I fell asleep on the sofa." He looked at his bare feet and was quiet for a moment. "She's still not home and the sun's nearly up." His voice was rough and cracked.

"I know. I can't sleep for thinking of it." Joe put his arms down and crossed them against this chest, which bore a Superman emblem on the front of his t-shirt. "I really hope she's safe."

The next morning, Jennifer woke up from the sofa to see Joe asleep in the armchair, with his shoes still on. They had waited until dawn for Katherine to come home, but had both eventually fallen asleep in the living room. The curtains were still drawn from the night before and the room was dark. She could see the dust in the sunbeams that leaked through the gap at the edge of the window.

She got up and shuffled into the bathroom. She stripped out of her tight clubbing dress and stepped into the shower. Jennifer let the water burn her for a moment before she turned the dial down to setting 5. She washed her hair and cleaned her body and then turned the water off. She picked up her towel from the floor and wrapped it around herself and walked out of the bathroom. Joe was in the kitchen making coffee; the smell nauseated her as she walked into her bedroom and locked the door behind her. She dried herself and searched for something to wear. Her jeans lay crumpled on the floor. Jennifer picked them up and put them on the bed while she looked for a top. Her skin dried in the heat of the room as she got dressed. When she got around to drying her hair, the scream of the hair-dryer was deafening in the flat.

Jennifer went back into the living room, where Joe sat glaring at a cup of coffee as if it was somehow responsible for his girlfriend's disappearance.

"Her phone's still off." He didn't look up at her but he knew she was there. His mobile phone was placed on the seat next to him, the lock screen showing a picture of him and Katherine at her birthday. *She looked so beautiful that night*, Jennifer thought.

"Maybe it ran out of battery. You know what she's like." The doubt rang out in her tone but she tried to cover it with a smile. Jennifer paced a little in the space behind the sofa, and then realised it was not only making her but Joe as well nervous, so she gave up and leaned against the arm of the sofa for a moment.

"She would have called." Joe turned to her with dread in his eyes. "Kat would have found a way to call one of us. Or she would have come home. It's nearly 11 a.m. for Christ's sake, she's hardly going to be asleep." He picked up his coffee and breathed in the steam. Jennifer sat down on the other side of the sofa. She could see he was trying to hold back the anger because his hands turned white as he gripped the mug.

"We can ring around the girls? They might have heard from her – she could have called someone to pick her up." She fiddled with the corner of the stripy cushion to the left of her. "If she couldn't get home then she probably just went home with a friend, right? We don't need to worry..."

"Yes, maybe." He drank his coffee.

"Okay, we can go round and look for her and if we have no luck, we can ring the police and file a missing persons report." She stood up fast and aimed for the kitchen. The kettle was already boiled; she fixed herself a cup of tea and leaned in the doorway between the two rooms.

****

Jennifer leant against the frame of the door. They were both silent for a moment and then Joe looked up at her. But he wasn't looking at her; he was looking for some sign of Katherine.

They were both still expecting her to waltz through the door with a whirlwind story of adventure and an explanation of where she had been all night. But it wouldn't happen. Jennifer knew in her heart that Katherine was gone and she would always be looking for her – in the crowd, in a line at the store, in the library, in the living room. The world would be constantly reminding her of things Katherine would love, or find funny. She would see Katherine in a strange woman walking down the street. They would both always be searching for Katherine.

"Do you think she's okay?" she asked, for something to say to fill the silence of the flat.

"To be honest? No." He walked off and sat on the sofa in the dark, head in his hands, his shoulders shaking as he sobbed. Jennifer shut her bedroom door and got back into bed, knowing that she wouldn't be able to sleep.

Jennifer and Joe were on edge and silent for the rest of the morning. They only muttered at each other, going about their preparations. Jennifer gathered photos of Katherine, her birth certificate, any form of identification she could find – things that might help the police. She printed out pictures from the night Katherine went missing, of her in her yellow dress, so that the police could correctly describe her on the night of her disappearance.

They had decided to wait until they had spoken to the police before they rang Katherine's parents. Jennifer agreed that they needed a plan before they divulged any information to anyone. They needed to be sure of what was going on.

Joe drove them to the police station at 1 p.m.: they sat in silence in the car. The man on the radio was talking about the best way to grow spring vegetables.

They arrived at the police station and got out of the car. They walked up the steps slowly, in no rush – neither of them wanted to hear what they were about to be told. Jennifer opened the door and held it for Joe, who nodded in appreciation. She walked up to the reception desk and a police officer approached them.

"Hello, my name is DI Johnson. Can I help you, ma'am?"

"Um, yes – my flatmate went missing at 2a.m on Saturday morning. We haven't seen her since."

"Why did you wait so long?" The officer was clearly annoyed by this. "Have you phoned around, checked she didn't stay somewhere else for the night?"

"Yes, we've called everyone." Jennifer held her breath.

"Okay, ma'am, sir, would you come into my office and we can talk about this properly" He picked up a white coffee-stained mug and escorted them to his office. He had a picture on his desk of two little girls, about six and nine years old. They were blonde and smiling, laughing at a forgotten joke.

"Right, what was her name?" He sat down at his desk and placed the mug to his left.

"Katherine Anna Luca."

"Her age?"

"Twenty-two."

"Physical description?"

"Actually, I have a photo of what she looked like the night she went missing."

"Oh, okay let's have it then." She offered him the picture of a 5'8 brunette in a yellow mini dress. "Thank you." He examined the image and filled out her physical description on the missing persons form.

"And where were you when she disappeared, Miss......?"

"I'm Jennifer Hampton."

"Okay Miss Hampton, where were you?"

"We were clubbing in town and I went to the bar to get us some drinks."

"Were there any other people with you on the night she disappeared?"

"No, it was just us on a night out."

"And where were you sir?"

"I was at home, watching TV."

"And can anyone vouch for that, sir – a girlfriend perhaps?"

"Katherine was my girlfriend. I was texting her up until about midnight when I fell asleep." Joe handed his phone over to the police officer. The officer scrolled through the phone for the text messages.

"Miss Hampton, could you fill out the details on this contact form – just so that I can get in touch with you in the light of any new information."

"Of course." Jennifer filled the form out carefully and placed it on the desk. The officer waited a moment before he spoke.

"Okay, here's what's going to happen. I'm going to send out this missing persons report to all the officers in the area, along with this photo of her on the night in question. We will interview anyone that is close to her – we will have to speak to her parents, her current place of work, you two and anyone who might have come into contact with her. We will check the nightclub for CCTV and we will speak to the bar staff and the bouncers who were on duty. We will do everything we can to find her." He had a sombre expression on his face. She could tell that this was not the first time he had had a missing persons case on his desk. It probably wouldn't be the last, either.

"But, the bouncers didn't even recognise her when I asked them last night – what makes you think they will remember her now?" asked Jennifer, exasperated with his response. She knew he was trying to help, but all she wanted to hear was the truth.

"Miss Hampton, I'm sure they will co-operate to the best of their ability." He was frustrated by her.

"But they didn't remember her!" Jennifer slammed her hand down on the desk that lay between the three of them. The officer didn't flinch.

"Officer, what are the chances of her coming home to us?"

"I won't lie to you: you've waited too long – the first few hours of these cases are crucial. But I won't know anything until I've got officers out there investigating."

"Is she dead?"

"We don't know anything yet. I can't say what her chances are."

"Officer, please. Do you think she is still alive?"

The officer breathed out hard and looked up from his desk. "She was taken, if she was taken, in a public area in the middle of the night. She is an attractive young female, she was intoxicated. From what you've told me – no one saw her being taken, which we will confirm with the external CCTV. This could, in all likelihood, be a kidnapping case. Has anyone tried to contact you?"

"No nothing like that." She wrung her hands together.

"Is there anyone that would have any reason to harm her – perhaps a jealous ex-boyfriend or a disgruntled colleague?"

"No, no one. Everyone loved her."

He sighed, "In that case, I would say it's probably random. It might have been another person from the club, who could have convinced her to go home with them and it ended badly. But we can't assume anything right now. I will get my best men on the case, Miss Hampton. In the meantime, go home and get some rest." The officer turned to Joe with a serious look on his face. "Sir, I'd like you to stay behind and answer a few questions."

"You think I did this?" The rage in his voice was like nothing Jennifer had ever heard before.

"Well sir, partners are always the first to be questioned in these cases, as that is often where the solution lies."

"I have to take Jennifer home first." He looked at her with tears in his eyes.

"Don't worry; I'll have Officer Carmen drive Miss Hampton home." The officer waved a man into the office. He was tall and thin, with sunglasses balanced on the top of his head.

"Carmen – could you drive this young lady home please?" The officer nodded and walked away.

"Jennifer, I will do everything I can to help you."

"Thanks." She walked out of the office.

Jennifer tried going to work straight after the disappearance, but she couldn't concentrate. She kept filing blank paper work and ignoring customers. She spent an entire hour trying to remember who William Shakespeare was and where he lived on their dusty store bookshelves. She had completely forgotten how to do anything other than wish that Katherine would come back. Nothing mattered any more – and it wouldn't until Katherine was back in her life. Her boss gave her time off, *"Take as much time as you need"*, he said. But she didn't care. She decided to take a few weeks just to stay at home and wait by the door. Everyone kept telling her to go back to work but she just sat drinking tea from Katherine's favourite mug and wearing her oversized jumpers. She ignored everyone's calls except Joe's and Katherine's parents.

When she had to phone Katherine's parents and tell them what was going on right after Katherine had been kidnapped, they knew already. There had been a news bulletin on local day time television to see if the general public had any information but it wasn't making a difference – no one had seen her. The only calls they got were to confirmed that they had seen Katherine and Jennifer enter the club together, but nobody reported seeing anyone else with them all night. Not even the CCTV footage was useful when they finally managed to get hold of it because it was too dark and Jennifer had stepped into a blind spot behind a solid banister. All you could see was her head bobbing along to the music and then her suddenly vanishing. No one is seen on camera approaching her, and everyone in the club had since been background checked and interviewed - everyone had cleared and no one remembered seeing Katherine leave. Jennifer still tried phoning her every day. No one ever answered. After a week, the phone battery died and it switched off. After two weeks, Jennifer had filled the voice-mail inbox with her cries and pleas for Katherine to be returned safely to her.

Chapter Six

Katherine opened her eyes when she heard the door open. She'd given up on her quest to escape after her captor had caught her trying to wriggle free of her cold, metal restraints. He bought strong handcuffs and cuffed her feet together so she couldn't walk very far. She could just about manage to hobble around her room for a couple of minutes before she would trip and fall. The seventeenth time she tried to hobble free when he was out, she fell and hit her head on the floor and ended up passing out. She woke up three days later and the man had chained her to the bed by her hands. She'd decided not to risk a concussion again - if only for a little while.

Instead, she started screaming at all hours of the night in the hope that some one would hear her cries and come and help her, but after three nights of screeching herself out of a voice, she gave up and the man decided to take action. Every time he left the building, he would force feed her a sleeping pill so she slept through his absence. If she refused to take the pill then he would dose her food or water. So she gave up resisting.

Soon, she was constantly in a state of confusion, were things real or was it all a dream? She wondered often if Jennifer and Joe were looking for her. It had crossed her mind that if they involved the police, they would probably blame Joe for it all. On the TV shows, they always say it's the boyfriend or the husband - they're the go-to criminal suspect. Katherine wished she could tell the world what really happened, but Man kept a close watch on here when he was there, and when he wasn't: she was drugged to within an inch of her sanity. She had no way of communicating with the outside world, and it was starting to take it's toll. Katherine wasn't even sure how long she had been imprisoned, whether it was days or weeks. Nothing made sense to her weak, drugged mind any more.

One day when she awoke from a particularly long drug-riddled nap, she found that not only had the man left and came back to the room but that he had brought things with him. Her eyes adjusted to the mid day light and she saw: a pile of new clothes and some shoes, a rug on the floor, bedding, books, DVDs and a TV/DVD player. He was trying to keep her entertained and quiet.

"What's all this?" She whispered drowsily.

"I thought it might keep you happy whilst I was out instead of screaming your head off or crying."

"You could just let me go?"

"I can't. You'll tell people what I did and who I am. I can't have you ruining things."

"You know I won't tell. I don't even know you're name."

"I don't have one. Not any more. Just keep calling me Man. At least I'm definitely a man."

"Thanks Man - for the stuff. At least my prison is in the same state as all those minimum security ones in the country now." She laughed dryly and then checked herself for conversing with the man who stole her from life and locked her up because he was trying to get to something, or someone - that much she could tell. After a while, she started to think that maybe Man had been after Jennifer instead. *After all, it had been dark in the club, and he seemed really confused when he saw me...* She thought. Katherine still couldn't figure out who he was, and if he was after Jennifer, he certainly wasn't an ex boyfriend or someone from their university. Jennifer and Katherine shared everything so she would have known. He obviously wasn't a relative otherwise he would have known what she looked like and wouldn't have taken the wrong person. Katherine couldn't understand how Man could be so obsessed with Jennifer - if that was who he was after -, but barely know anything about her adult life other than anything that could be gleaned from her social media or a quick Google search. He didn't know her now, that much Katherine had figured out. But why he searching for Jennifer was a question she couldn't answer without delving deeper into the mind of her kidnapper, which was something she was trying to avoid with her best efforts.

Katherine wasn't even sure it was Jennifer that he was really after, but her instincts told her otherwise and she felt it her duty to protect her friend for as long as she could.

Chapter Seven

After multiple interrogations and alibi conformations, the police finally released Joe days later without any charges and they were still no closer to finding Katherine. He drove home as the sun started to set, his stomach rumbling and his eyes raw from crying. He blasted music from his iPod in an attempt to block out his anger but it only made him worse. He started to feel furious as he drove down the main junction to get home. *Why do they suspect me? Just because I'm her boyfriend? I wanted to marry her not kill her. It doesn't make any sense, why would anyone do this? She's an innocent young woman, she's never hurt anyone. It just doesn't make any sense. And I don't look like a killer, do I? I'm a nice guy – I'm a businessman for god's sake, I'm hardly the criminal type!* Joe turned left and headed up another main road, his driving was perfect despite his clouded mind. *I need to do something, the police are being useless... not even looking in the right places. Katherine said I was always great in a crisis... maybe I should look for her? Yeah – that's what I'll do. I'll look for her myself. It can't cause any harm, surely the more people searching, the better?*

He pulled up outside his building and got out of the car. He slammed the door just to expel some of the anger and then he climbed the six flights of stairs to his flat. It was clean and spacious, if somewhat empty. His furniture all matched and was all quite expensive. But the tell-tale signs of a man in his twenties who lived alone were the empty pizza boxes and the gadgets. He had a gadget for everything. Joe had it all: tablets, smart-phones, laptops, netbooks, PCs, state-of-the art kitchen, huge flat screen TVs, a High-Definition music system – everything. He had worked hard for it too. His business degree hung pride of place on the living room's feature wall and it was the only picture frame, other than the picture of him and Katherine at his cousin's wedding that, he ever dusted. The rest of his pictures gracefully gathered dust and faded into the background. But his degree and the picture of the two of them together shone on the magnolia walls. Joe placed his keys on the small nested tables by the front door and grabbed himself a beer from the kitchen. It was imported from Germany and he could barely understand the labels, but it was good beer and was perfect for taking the edge of a hard day. In the business world, Joe was still a nobody but he had big dreams. He didn't just want to own one company, but dozens. The plan was to work his way from the ground up and then eventually take over the company he now worked in. He was already ahead of schedule with favourable talk from the board of directors talking him up to 'the big bosses'. Since he got the job he had already been promoted twice in just a few months and was now heading his own division. The next stop was company management. Joe was good at what he did and he worked hard every day, but since Katherine vanished he hadn't gone to work. He had barely explained what was happening to his boss before he had to go in for more questioning. It was the weekend so he took take a few days to relax, but the impending doom of having to show up for work on Monday morning and explain what had happened was starting to stress him out. Joe swigged from the bottle, collapsing on the sofa and switching the TV on with his universal remote. It controlled several devices in the living room including the music and gaming systems and some of the overhead spot lights. Joe held the remote in his hand and thought about how Katherine was always talking about how confusing all the buttons were. He smiled, but then the remote just reminded him that he couldn't control what was happening: he couldn't just push a button and rewind to a time when he still had Katherine in his life. This thought confirmed his plans, and it stayed with him.

On Monday morning, Joe marched into work and after a quick meeting with the bosses – who were all supportive of his situation – he called a small team of his staff into his office and told them his plans. Jones' – Joe's right hand man - had a brother who was a private detective and Jones' offered his services. Everyone was eager to help him find Katherine, and with that – his search began.

Chapter Eight

Katherine's parents stayed in a local hotel while they went through her belongings together. Jennifer couldn't understand how they could do it – go through her things as if they were organising a car boot sale, not laying bare someone's life. She wanted to keep all of it: every single scrap of paper, every item of clothing, her perfume, her memory. In her mind, going through Katherine's things was like packing up someone's life even though they were going to come right back. They took her childhood belongings, photos and such and a few photos from her life with Jennifer – but they gave Jennifer the rest to do with what she wanted. They gave her Katherine's clothes: they couldn't tell whose clothes belonged to whom because the girls had always shared a sense of style, if only ironically. Jennifer spent a day going through what was left of Katherine's things in the apartment, deciding what she could cope with keeping and what needed to go. She couldn't stand to see her best friend's things being left in storage to be forgotten and gather dust. She took reusable belongings to charity shops. She kept the photos and mementos of their friendship, swearing secretly to herself that this division was only temporary.

Katherine's parents covered the next month's rent while Jennifer tried to find somewhere else to live. But she couldn't bring herself to look for either a new flat or a new flatmate. Joe offered his sofa for a few days while she got on her feet, but she couldn't bear the idea of spending so much time with Joe, without her. It was Joe himself who stopped her from accepting his offer, whether he knew it or not. Every time she saw him, she felt a deep sense of responsibility for all of this. Jennifer knew that she wasn't to blame for Katherine's disappearance, but she still felt guilty.

Despite their best efforts, Katherine's parents could do nothing right in Jennifer's confused mind. They took her stuff, they took her home: everything that made the apartment home was Katherine's - and it was all gone. She felt alone and cold there, so she spent as little time at home as possible. She went for walks, she visited work, she took a book to the park and spent all day there. She tried visiting friends but they were either acting like Katherine was dead, or acting as if Jennifer had lost her mind with grief. But she wasn't grieving: she was waiting.

Jennifer went back to work a month later but she didn't feel at home in the book store any more. Its warmth had cooled for her; the glowing darkness of the book-store had morphed into confusing lighting. The overhead lights glared at her as she got on with her work. On her lunch break, Jennifer went to her usual coffee place and sat in the corner with a large tea in an attempt to recover some normality. The smell of coffee was usually a comfort to Jennifer, but now it made her feel sick in the pit of her stomach. She tried to hold her breath to stop the coffee entering her lungs, but it didn't help. Her eyes bore into her cooling tea, her hands wrapped around the mug in a failed attempt to try to warm her. Everything felt blurred, as if the world was darkening around her, suffocating her and she couldn't escape it.

Jennifer took a sip of her tea and as she looked over her mug she saw Marcus, the man she met there before all this happened, ordering his drink. He scanned the room for a seat and saw her sitting in the corner. He picked up his drink and walked over to her with a friendly grin on his face.

"Is it okay to sit here?" Marcus gestured to the armchair opposite her.

"Um, yes of course." She fumbled with the handle of the mug.

"Remember me, Marcus?"

"Yeah," she faked a smile, because even in her grieving state - she was still a polite member of society who believed she should be friendly to everyone until they gave her a reason not to. Also, she found him rather attractive.

"Jennifer, right?" she nodded in response. "How are you?" Marcus asked, fiddling with his coffee cup.

She paused for a moment before responding, "Awful actually. It's my first day back at work in a while." Jennifer bit her lip, thinking that she should just politely make an excuse and leave early. But something about Marcus made her stay where she was.

"Post-holiday blues?" He asked, stirring the coffee.

"Oh, no," she stumbled over her words, "my best friend's missing."

"Oh, fuck – I'm so sorry. What happened, if you don't mind my asking?" He bit his lip and leaned forward slightly.

"She was kidnapped. We were on a night out and.... she was gone." She rubbed her eyes and dragged her hands down her face. She started crying quietly.

"I'm sorry – I shouldn't have asked." He put his hand on the table.

"No, no," she sobbed, choking back tears, "It's fine, it's just – no one has asked me."

"Surely that's a good thing?"

She sobbed again, "They blame me."

"What?"

"We were out just the two of us. I shouldn't have left her alone. I shouldn't..." Her voice cracked as she ran her hands into her hair, gripping and pulling at it while she rocked in the armchair. Her elbows rested firmly on the table; supporting her as her life crumbled from underneath her. Marcus gently took her hands from her hair and held them. He whispered, "Its okay," over and over again until she remembered how to breathe. "I'm so lonely without her."

"Can't you talk to your boyfriend? Your house-mates?"

"She," Jennifer sniffed, "she was my house-mate." She cried, mentally wondering when she had she had become such an emotional wreck. It could have been so much worse - Katherine could be dead. *I know she's only missing but it feels like she's gone. I just want her to come back.*

"Oh, fuck. I can't stop putting my foot in it today, can I?" Jennifer looked up at him and his sad smile. His expression made her laugh.

"What?" he asked.

"I must look a mess to you."

"I don't mind."

The moment of glee escaped her instantly. "Ugh and I need to move house now and I can't live with any of our friends because all they do is ask me if I'm okay and then they tell me I need to move on." She looked him in the eyes, "I can't move on yet because I won't except it. She's missing, not dead. They keep acting like she's dead..." her voice trailed off.

"Well, you shouldn't have to. Can't you stay in your house?"

"No, it's too much."

He looked down for a moment.

"What?" Her eyebrows drew together.

"Look, I know you don't even know me, but I think I might be able to help you out."

"What do you mean?" she sniffed again.

He sat back in his seat, "My house-mate just got engaged and he's moving in with the girl – nice girl, if a bit dim. Anyway, I've got a spare room and I need to fill it. I'm not usually one to ask strangers, but all my friends are already living with people and you seem nice enough."

"Are you serious? Well – where is it?" She wiped her nose on her sleeve.

"Just ten minutes walk away from here." Marcus glanced at his watch, "Look – I have to get back to work – here is my number." He scrawled his mobile number on the back of a napkin. "Call me later if you feel like having a look at the place." He looked up at the tear-stained woman in front of him. "Or if you just need a chat." He stood up and finished his coffee, buttoning his coat.

"Thank you so much. Seriously – you've no idea."

"No problem, Jennifer." He smiled at her.

"I'll call you tonight, if that's okay."

"Go for it." He grinned and walked away.

***

Jennifer went home after work and drew herself a bath to try and relieve the stress, but it didn't work. Her whole body was tense; no matter how she stood, how she lay, what she took – the pain wouldn't stop. She let the steaming water soak her to the bone; the bubbles attached to her skin, the floral aroma from the soaps making her feel dizzy. Jennifer's mobile phone buzzed on the bathroom floor, she dried her hands with the towel beside it and answered the phone: it was Joe.

"Hey, what's up?"

"Err, not a lot. Sorry – did I disturb you?" Joe's detached voice echoed around the bathroom.

"No – it's fine. I'm in the bath." There was an awkward silence for a moment.

"Erm, right... anyway – the reason I called is that I still really think you should move in with me whilst you –"

"Oh, I meant to text you. I've found somewhere."

"I thought you said all the girls already have house-mates."

"They do. It's not one of the girls. It's not even a girl, actually." She brushed the bubbles away from her face.

"Well, who is it?" His voice harshened.

"It's a guy I met in the coffee shop ages ago. I had a bit of a breakdown at lunch today and he was there. He's really nice, his name's Marcus."

"What and he just asked you to live with him?"

"No, I told him I needed somewhere and he said his flatmate is moving in with his girlfriend so if I wanted to, I could check the place out."

"And you're going to?"

"Well what choice do I have? I'm going to call him later and arrange to see the place tomorrow."

"Do you want me to come with you?" The concern rang out in his tone.

"No, I'll be fine."

"Are you sure, I mean this guy is a stranger?"

"What is it with you?" Jennifer barked at him.

"Nothing, nothing. Sorry, long day. I've been at the police station with that DI. again."

Jennifer sat up in the bath and the water splashed about her. "What? Why? Did they find a new lead?"

"No, Jen. They're calling it off. She's been missing for too long. They say that we are welcome to keep looking for her and that they will do what they can, but that it would be best for everyone if we just moved on."

"But –" she gasped.

"I've spoken to her parents and they agree. They want to hold a memorial service in her honour."

"But there's no body because she's not dead. We can't have a funeral..." she drew her knees to her chest and rocked gently back and forth.

"Memorial service," he corrected her bluntly.

"...without a body." She paused for a moment to catch her breath. "How can you be okay with this?"

"Because she's gone, Jen. It's over." he answered her curtly, but he spoke as if they were not his words. He had been seeing a therapist, so she assumed this sudden need for closure was their doing and nothing to do with whether Katherine was actually alive or not.

"I won't stop looking for her" she yelped.

"I know." Joe sounded clipped, but even in her rage Jennifer could tell that he was fighting back the tears as much as she was.

Jennifer hung up the phone and threw it across the room. It bounced off the white-tiled wall and landed on her clothes. She sank underneath the water and stayed there until it went cold.

Chapter Nine

Jennifer had arranged to meet Marcus outside the coffee shop after she finished work. *He seems nice enough*, she thought. She stood underneath her damp, broken umbrella as she waited. After a few minutes, she started to think he wasn't going to show up at all, until he walked around the corner and flashed a smile. She wrapped her coat around her a little more and began to walk over to Marcus. As she did, a gust of wind stole her umbrella and slammed it to the ground. The metal arms reached unnaturally through the black fabric and she stood staring at the wrecked umbrella as the water started to soak her skin. Marcus ran over and put his umbrella over her head. *He's a lot taller than I remember*, she noted.

"Hi. Here, take mine. I've got a hood."

"Are you sure?"

"Yeah, go for it. We can't have you catching a cold." He smiled at her and handed her the umbrella. They walked back around the corner from which Marcus had just emerged and journeyed towards his apartment.

"So, is your flatmate still there, or -"

"Oh, no – he's moved out now. You'd think he never lived there – his room is so clean!" They laughed and walked up the high street.

"How far is it?" Jennifer shifted the umbrella from one hand to the other.

"About five minutes away if we walk fast enough." Marcus looked over his shoulder and then turned back, gently touching her upper arm. "Actually – let's get a cab. I can't be bothered with the rain tonight." He took her hand and pulled her towards the taxi rank across the street. Jennifer climbed into the back of the black taxi while Marcus spoke to the driver. Then he climbed in next to her.

The taxi smelled of dust and plastic, making Jennifer feel dizzy. The driver took them to Marcus' apartment, winding through back streets to avoid the traffic caused by the dismal weather. When they arrived, Marcus paid the taxi driver, despite Jennifer's protest and they got out of the taxi. The building was new, but made to look as if it was built in the Tudor era. It was stark white with shining black beams and a great oak door. The only sign of modernism to the front of the house was a satellite dish and the intercom. Marcus led her to the entrance and pulled out his keys.

"It's beautiful. I have no idea how I'm going to afford this!" Jennifer stated in awe as Marcus turned the key. They walked inside and were greeted by a black and white spiral staircase in the middle of the foyer. There was a door either side of the great room, with the numbers '1' and '2' in shining silver.

"I'm '2' - I could have had '3' which is bigger, but I couldn't be bothered with the stairs – I've wasted a day laughing at removal men trying to get sofas and things down those stairs." He smiled again and walked over to his flat. Jennifer followed behind, looking around the great foyer. *This place looks like it's worth more than my entire flat and it's basically just a corridor* she thought, as she jogged to catch up with him and entered the apartment, closing the door behind her.

The apartment was as grand as the rest of the building, with high ceilings and beautiful artwork everywhere. It was clean and modern. Jennifer felt at home when she saw the kitchen. There were glass cupboards and one was full of about fifty different kinds of tea.

"You like tea then?" she peered in from the doorway.

"Yes." He smiled and stepped out of her way so she could look at the rest of the kitchen. It was narrow, but big enough to cook in. The black floor tiles glittered under her feet and the whole kitchen was spotless.

"Would you like to see your room?"

"Yeah, okay," she smiled at him, his hair, damp from the rain, made him look younger than she suspected he really was. "Lead the way."

Marcus led her out of the kitchen and around the corner to a varnished oak door. He unlocked and opened it, allowing Jennifer to walk in. The room was bright, with two windows and overhead lighting. The furniture was all black painted wood with white and silver decorations dotted around the room.

"Wow. It's like a picture from a magazine."

"It's the IKEA Summer catalogue actually." His voice came from behind her; a sarcastic playfulness rang out in his tone. She turned around to face him and found him standing closer than she realised. Her hand brushed his arm and they both shivered.

"I must be colder than I thought." She looked at her feet and ignored the moment. "So, how much is it?"

"£350 a month, including bills." He laughed at Jennifer as her mouth fell open.

"Are you kidding me?"

"No." He winked at her.

"£350 – that's all? I'm paying more than that now!"

"Want it then?"

"Of course!" She laughed. *At least I've got a place to live now,* she thought, soaking in the first time she had felt happy in over a month.

"Shall we celebrate? I've got a bottle of wine in the fridge."

"Sounds like a plan." Marcus took Jennifer to the living room. There were two large black leather sofas and a fluffy white rug in the centre of the room. There was a large electric fire and above that, a 40 inch flat screen TV. *This place is incredible, why is it so cheap?* she thought, sitting down on the bigger of the two sofas.

"Did somebody die here?" Jennifer asked Marcus as he walked out of the kitchen holding two wine glasses.

"Err – no. What makes you say that?"

"Well, it's a beautiful place, why isn't the landlord charging more?"

Marcus handed her a glass, "Because there is no landlord. It's my apartment."

"You own this place and you only want £350 from me?"

"I didn't want to charge loads, I don't need to. I earn enough to live here by myself; I just like having someone to come home to." He took a sip of his wine. He looked up to see Jennifer blushing and smiling into her drink.

"Mm, this wine is delicious."

"Thanks, I have a friend who makes it. I buy twelve bottles a year from him. Costs me £1000 but it's worth it."

"A grand? You paid a grand for wine?"

"For twelve bottles of wine, not one. That would just be insane." He chuckled and held up his glass. "A toast."

"To what?" she giggled.

He paused and then looked her straight in the eyes, "To a long and happy friendship."

"Indeed, cheers!" They clinked their glasses and sipped their wine.

Chapter Ten

Jennifer stood in her empty bedroom and sighed. Today was the day she moved out of her apartment, just two months after Katherine was kidnapped. She checked the room one last time and then closed the door behind her. The living room was bare except for some furniture; the character of the room was gone. There was no artwork on the walls, or half-finished cups of tea on the coffee table. Just a clean, empty, lifeless apartment that she was about to leave forever. *It's only an apartment,* she thought, *I can do this.* Jennifer picked up the last box from the end of the sofa and replaced it with her keys. Marcus walked in and took the box from her.

"Ready to go, babe?"

"Yeah," she shrugged a little and Marcus put the box down. He walked over to her and gave her a hug, holding her tight as she sobbed onto his shoulder.

"You don't have to leave, you know. I could pay for this place …"

"No, I have to go. Staying here just reminds me of her." She hugged him back and then moved away. "Can I have a minute? I need to leave the landlord a forwarding address." She smiled at her boyfriend and nodded, letting him know it was okay to leave her alone. Jennifer had been emotional all week as they had packed up the apartment and prepared to move her into Marcus' place. She kept going from ecstatic to miserable on a daily basis, which was made even worse when she had found a box of Katherine's clothes in a cupboard.

"Yes, sure – I'll meet you downstairs." Marcus kissed her on the forehead and then walked out. Jennifer closed the door behind him and then tore a sheet of paper from the memo pad by the phone and jotted down her new address, with strict instructions to send all post there, and if Katherine ever showed up to call her immediately. She pinned the note to the cork-board on the wall and turned back to face the inside of the apartment.

"Oh, Kat, I wish you were here to meet him. He's a star. It's like I've been hit over the head with feelings. You always told me Mr. Right was out there and sure enough I've met him and we're moving in together. You would have loved him; he's kind, he really cares about me. He drives me everywhere… I need to learn to drive, but Marcus thinks it would be too much for me right now. He's right, ah Kat – he's always right. Bless him, I love him so much. It's crazy, I've not even known him for very long, but we just…connected. I haven't told him yet, but I think he knows. We haven't kissed or anything either, it's that part before the good stuff, when everything feels tingly." She sniffed, unaware she was crying.

"Katherine I miss you! Come back, please. I don't know what I'm supposed to do without you." She collapsed, sliding down the door, holding her head in her hands. A pain seared through her head as tears escaped her eyes. After a moment, she took a deep breath and calmed herself. A voice echoed in the hallway outside the door.

"Jen, are you alright?" He knocked on the door when she didn't answer him. "Jennifer? Are you okay?" He knocked.

She sniffed and opened the door to let him in. Marcus took one look at her wet eyes and pulled her close.

"Oh, honey, come here – what happened?" He stroked her hair.

"I was saying goodbye to…" She sobbed and collapsed against him, her arms around his neck were the only things stopping her from hitting the ground. "I needed to…" she broke off as the tears stole her voice. Jennifer nuzzled her face into his shirt, letting mascara ruin the blue cotton.

"It's okay, she's not really gone. You loved her and she will stay with you forever. Haunting you like a ghost." Jennifer giggled and pulled back so she could see his face.

"Marcus?" she looked into his eyes as he wiped away her tears.

"Yeah?" a concerned look crossed his face.

"I…" she stopped her words and closed her eyes, taking a deep breath. She opened her eyes again and looked up at him. She touched the side of his face with her fingers, tracing his cheekbone. She pulled his face to hers and kissed him. And he kissed her back. Their bodies pressed together as they embraced; his hand on her back pulling her closer, her arms around his neck, drawing him in. They let go of each other.

"Jen, you're upset. You're going through something huge –." Jennifer kissed him again and he stopped talking. She pushed him against the strip of wall beside the door and kept on kissing him. His body relaxed and he pulled her closer, running his hands through her hair. Jennifer pulled back.

"Do I look upset any more?" she poked her tongue out at him and grinned.

Marcus breathed out, his eyes shining. "No, you look happy."

"I am happy, I've got you." She stepped back and smoothed down her hair. "Now, let's get out of here." She grabbed his hand and pulled him out of the apartment, leaving behind her life and her search for Katherine.

****

"That's it, that's the last box." Marcus called from the front door of their apartment. "Now you've got to unpack it all." He laughed, wiping the sweat from his brow. He took off his shoes and placed them on the shoe rack by the door.

"I'll do it later, I need a drink." Jennifer walked into the kitchen and took a mug from one of the plastic boxes. She removed the day-old newspaper and filled the mug with water. Taking a sip, the heat started to leave her body. She was covered in sweat from moving all of the boxes from the van to her new room. She walked out into the living room holding the mug in her right hand, her left hand on her hip. "It's not like I'm in a rush to unpack, most of my essential stuff is all in the same suitcase."

"That's useful." Marcus padded over to her.

She murmured, drinking the water. "I'm a good packer. I'm great on holiday; everything has its own part of the suitcase." Jennifer smiled and reached up to kiss him. Marcus put his hands over her mouth.

"Not until you've unpacked at least your suitcase." She giggled at him and shrugged her shoulders.

"Do I have to?" she whined into her drink.

"Yes." He winked at her and stole her mug, taking a sip and strolled into her bedroom. It was full of boxes, but the room was large so there was still space to manoeuvre across the box-littered floor. He picked his way around the room until he got to the queen-sized bed in its centre. He opened her suitcase and stared at the neatly arranged contents. "Wow, you are organised." He laughed, "So where is your bedding?" he started taking items out of the case: a wash bag, a hair brush, a photo frame and placed them on the bedside table. He looked up when Jennifer didn't answer. "What?"

Jennifer stared at him from the door, embarrassed; "I need to buy new bedding."

"Why?" he asked, puzzled.

"My bedding's not going to fit that bed – I had a double, that thing," she pointed to the bed "is the same size as my entire room was!" She sighed, letting the hot air leave her mouth.

"Well then, let's go shopping." Marcus grinned, pulling her by the hand out of the room. He put the mug in the kitchen and then headed for the shoe rack. She stayed in the doorway, staring at him, frustration mixed with amusement etched into her eyes. He walked back over to her. "What's wrong?"

"I can't afford –." Marcus put his hand on her mouth.

"My treat. Come on, shoes on – let's go." He went and put his shoes on and Jennifer did as she was told.

"You're very bossy, you know that, right?" she pretended to strop at him, mockingly crossing her arms like a stubborn toddler.

"Yes, it's one of my best qualities. Let's go – we're wasting valuable shopping time!" He walked out of the apartment and Jennifer dutifully chased after him.

Chapter Eleven

Katherine couldn't stop thinking about how Man could know Jennifer - if he knew her at all. But she couldn't figure out if he had been in close contact with her, or if he was one of those creepy guys with binoculars that you see in the movies. He certainly didn't dress like a stalker, and on more than one occasion she had caught him getting changed from a suit into his jeans and t shirt. Katherine had a lot of time to think whilst Man locked her away in the dingy flat and she had often wondered if Man had a day job. *He could be a completely normal person and this is like his fetish or something, he could be an office worker and we're just his hobby! A sick, twisted, illegal hobby! Like some people join sports teams or knit - but instead he kidnaps and stalks young women.* After months of watching him, she had noticed a few things that were somewhat alarming. Firstly, he was easily confused and sometimes he spoke to himself, but as if he was speaking to a friend. She heard the name Jack mentioned a few times and considered that it could be his real name. However, she was smart enough to also consider the possibility that Man knew she could hear him, and was just trying to mess with her head.

One night, Man came home from what Katherine could only assume was his day job, carrying a briefcase and donning a smart three piece suit. She cursed herself for thinking that he looked somewhat attractive. It was a thought she had frequently and it upset her. It was hard to ignore how pretty he was, but then he usually tightened her restraints or stole her things, so it set him back to being the cruel crazy man who kidnapped her and kept her prisoner. On this particular night he looked happy, if a little distracted. Katherine realised this would be the perfect time to start interrogating him. She quickly tidied herself up and smoothed her hair down and shuffled into the living room where he sat, still in his suit. Man didn't acknowledge her as she entered the room, even though the rattling of her restraints echoed around the room as she moved.

"Hello. You look nice." She said, trying to force a friendly tone. Katherine sat down on a wooden chair to the left of him, and tried not to look him in the eye.

"Thanks. I'm not staying long, I've got to get home. I just wanted to make sure you had enough food and everything."

"Yes, lots of food - all stocked up, thanks." She paused for a moment before deciding to just go for it and start subtly questioning him. "Man?" Katherine sweetened her voice a little, as if she was about to ask him for a favour.

"Yeah?" he replied, cautious of his prisoner, but not enough to look at her. He often avoided looking at her face and sometimes Katherine thought it might be because he was pretending he hadn't stolen the wrong woman, and he was trying to pretend he was living his fantasy life with someone else, maybe even Jennifer. Katherine knew she had to get some information from him if she was going to figure out his motives.

"Do you have a real life? Like a job and a house and a family?" Katherine couldn't imagine him at home playing with his kids or having inside jokes with his work colleagues. Although he looked normal most of the time, he certainly didn't behave it - especially when he thought he was alone.

"Yes." He continued with his monosyllabic answers in the hope it would deter Katherine from asking him anything else, but at last he caved when she hit a nerve.

"Do they know about me?" she tilted her head as she spoke.

"No. And they're never going to." Man replied, concentrating on a mysterious stain on the opposite wall.

"It must be a really good job." Katherine twisted her ankle round so the chains made a clanking noise as she moved. She saw Man jump at the sound and smiled secretly to herself at this small success.

"What makes you think that?" He leaned back in his chair, almost as if he was allowing Katherine a better look at his attire. He had one long leg crossed over the other, and for a split second he reminded Katherine of Jack Skeleton from the children's film *Nightmare Before Christmas*. A spindly, confident yet confusing, hollowed man in a stripy black suit.

"Well, you dress quite well, and you don't seem poor. All the food you buy might be junk food, but it's high end. So you must make a lot of money. And, the fact that you are paying for this place as well as your family home: it just proves that you earn a lot of money." She shrugged as she said the last sentence in the hope that it might make her seem more casual about her statement than she actually was. But Man wasn't fooled.

"I do make a lot of money, yes. But I don't pay for this place anymore." He spoke slowly, but sill avoided looking at her. Instead he gazed around the room staring at wet wallpaper and a broken fireplace. The room was chilly and damp, just like the rest of the apartment. Katherine couldn't imagine the apartment ever being a home, it looked as it had been built for kidnappers to keep their prisoners in. It was dark, cold, daunting and unfriendly. Even traces of a normal life seemed eery: the random dirt-trodden strips of carpet looked as if it was once a bright orange and black pattern, a poor choice, but homely in a 1970's décor.

"Why not?" Katherine grew more curious with every response, but she tried to contain it. She didn't want to frighten her kidnapper into shutting up.

"It was my parent's apartment when I was a kid. I grew up here. When they died, I inherited it and paid off the mortgage. I was just using it for storage but then I saw Jennifer was living in town and, well, my motives changed."

"So, you didn't know she lived here?" Something in the back of her mind starting setting off alarm bells, but she kept a calm façade and tried to pay attention to the conversation.

"No." Man looked at her cautiously and asked, "why?"

"Well - we've lived in that apartment ever since we finished university." Katherine regretted saying anything. She felt like she was betraying Jennifer by talking to Man about their life together.

"When was that?" he demanded.

"Uh, three or four years?" Katherine replied, but on the inside she was panicking. *He doesn't know anything about her. If he didn't know we lived here, then he doesn't know that we went to university here. So where does he know her from? Does he even know her or am I just jumping to conclusions...?*

"I need to go." He jumped up from his seat, grabbing his briefcase as he swept out of the door. Katherine felt pleased that she had been able to rattle him so easily, but then she returned to worrying about Jennifer. Man's jumpiness confirmed that he knew Jennifer, which sent Katherine's mind spiralling as she tried to piece things together. This man obviously knew her when she was younger - that much was clear. But by the way he reacted to information about Jennifer's adult past, it seemed that he had a particular way he wanted Jennifer to be and if what he learned didn't fit that then he was upset and careless with his words. Katherine knew that unnerving him would be the best way to distract him enough so that he might leave her with an escape route. This time she had not been lucky enough as she could hear him locking the door after he had left, the keys and chains tinkling and chinking on the other side of the door.

Katherine withdrew to her bedroom/cell and shut the door in an attempt at vague privacy, but as she entered the room she realised something Man had said. *He grew up here. He played in this room - hell, he probably slept in this room. His parents tucked him into bed here and read him stories. Did he want to bring Jennifer here and try and force her to be some stereotypical house wife who tidies the house just before the husband gets home, and who frets about trivial things like how she looks and where exactly to buy the groceries from?* She leaned against the slightly damp wall and let her body slide down it until she hit the floor. She sat there for hours, long after the sun went down and tried to think about what Jennifer was doing at the precise moment. She hoped she was happy and getting on with life, but she secretly wished that Jennifer hadn't forgotten her after all this time.

Chapter Twelve

Jennifer picked up the photo of her and Katherine at their graduation and dusted underneath it, then placed it back down on the shelf. *It feels like you've been gone for years, not six months. I miss you Kat - where are you? Why haven't you come home?* she thought. She carried on dusting, a five-month-old Golden Retriever nipping at her ankles, a smile plastered onto her face followed by freshly done make up with scarlet lips to match her carefully chosen outfit. She was wearing black skin-tight jeans with a red loose floral top. It flowed and fluttered as she moved around the room. It was dainty, but low cut with a deep V-shaped neckline that reached her cleavage. Her shoes were matt black and six inches high, adding a significant height to her average size.

"Luca – shoo. Get away, boy. I'm trying to clean before Daddy's home from his business trip." The puppy yelped at her until she bent down to fuss over it. "I know, puppy. I miss him too. But he needs to work to look after us." She ruffled his fur, "Yes he does! Now," she pushed the dog gently away from her ankles, "leave me be. I'm busy." She picked up a deserted chew toy and threw it across the room and the dog scampered after it. When she finished her dusting, she plumped the cushions on the sofa, swept the floors and wiped the coffee table clean. Jennifer stood back, proud of her work. At that moment, Marcus unlocked the front door and she quickly glanced around the room to make sure everything was perfect. And it was, just like a picture of a model home from one of those thick, glossy magazines where all the women are stay-at-home moms but with a comfy work-from-homes jobs. They always look as perfect and pristine as their expensive homes. Jennifer smoothed her hair and quickly tucked a loose strand behind her ear.

"Hey Jen." He looked around the apartment "Wow – very nice. Five stars!" He winked at her and put his things down. He winced as he took off his long black overcoat, being careful not to move too fast.

"Oh, what's wrong?" Jennifer tottered over to him, not used to the height of her shoes, and touched him on the arm. He leant his weight on her a little and waited for the pain to stop.

"Aha, sitting at a desk all day is hardly good for your back." He straightened up as his lower back clicked and kissed Jennifer on the cheek.

"Neither is golf, dear." She smiled weakly, the worry creasing her eyes, but then she changed the conversation. "Luca is house-trained now." She smiled and stepped back, waiting for his approval, gesturing to the over-excited puppy chasing its own tail in the corner of the room. Luca had a habit of misbehaving at the exact moment Marcus walked through the door. He had been well-behaved, if a little bit annoying, all day. Jennifer checked herself for not asking the dog trainer how to stop it, and decided to ask him the next time she bumped into him on her way to town.

"How did you manage that in a week?" He took his black leather shoes off, leaning his back against the wall.

"That Spanish dog trainer down the road, he did it. Took him away for a few days, came back and Luca was as good as gold." She moved his shoes from the floor to the shoe rack.

"Nice." He sat down on the cold leather sofa and put his feet on the coffee table.

"He's still running around my ankles though." She frowned and crossed the room to Marcus. The puppy continued to spin itself dizzy in the corner, but was quiet all the same.

"You don't pay any attention to him, that's why. We've talked about this, Jen. He's here to keep you company when I'm at work. I'm away too much for you to just ignore him. You must start spending more time with him during the day." He rubbed his temples, his eyes scrunched closed. "Can you get me some water, please?"

"Of course." Jen jumped up from the sofa and rushed into the kitchen, being careful not to scuff the polished floor with her new shoes. She prepared the water and then grabbed some pain killers. She tapped back across the living room with a glass of water and handed it to Marcus. He drank the water and stared at her feet, making sure he didn't move his head suddenly.

"Why are you wearing high heels indoors?" he said scornfully as he swallowed the tablets.

"Don't you like them?" Jennifer pouted and went to remove them, but Marcus grabbed her wrist and pulled her onto his lap so her legs were on one side of him. She wriggled until she was comfortable and then proceeded to rub his temples for him.

"Why are you wearing them?" his voice deepened, his eyes closed.

"I thought you might like them. And, they help when I'm dusting." Marcus scoffed at her and then returned his attention to the glass of water in his right hand, the cold glass just grazing Jennifer's thigh.

"They're cute. But no one is going to see you in them other than me," he stated, sipping his water.

"I know…" Jennifer paused, deciding whether to ask.

"What?" he put the glass down on the coffee table and softened his voice. "You know you can tell me anything." He cupped her hands in his.

"I… I was thinking about going back to work next week." She lowered her gaze and dropped her hands so they touched his shoulders. "I bumped into my old boss and he said I was welcome back any time. He even offered me a pay rise." She swallowed, trying to smile.

"Why do you want to go back to work? We don't need the money." His tone dismissed her, but his face still smiled. He grabbed her hands.

"Well, it's something to do, instead of staying home all the time," she defended, trying to move her hands away from his but he didn't let go.

"Jen…" Marcus licked his lips and stared at their hands. "I know it's only been six months and I know a lot has happened this year and…"

"What?" she meowed.

"Sometimes, I feel like I pressured you into this relationship and that you don't love me."

"What? I do love you, I swear. It's just sometimes when you aren't here it's really lonely and…" she started whimpering as her mind raced ahead of the conversation. She was convinced he was about to break up with her.

"What if I were here more?" He bit his lip, stroking his thumb across the back of her hand.

"But, you can't be - you have to work." She sighed, her forehead wrinkling.

"I can start working from home for some of it – I can be with you and Luca?" He grazed her left cheek with his fingertips and kissed her right cheek. He felt her smile. Marcus pulled back and smiled. He lifted her gently from his lap and placed her sitting as he was standing up and going over to his suitcase, leaving Jennifer alone on the sofa. "I wasn't going to do this now, but it feels right." He pulled a small, cubed, red velvet box from the front pocket and carried it over to her, turning it in his hands as if it was a tennis ball.

"What's that?" Her eyes shone with the ignored tears of her loneliness and the joy of what was about to happen. She shifted in her seat to face him. Marcus knelt on the floor beside her.

"Jennifer, I know it's only been six months, but they have been the best six months of my life. We've been through so much together and I think that despite the bad times that brought us close, we should be grateful that we had each other." He opened the red box to reveal a glittering engagement ring. "Will you do me the honour of becoming my wife?" He paused, biting his lip, waiting for her response. Jennifer looked down at the ring, a large blue sapphire embedded in the top. She met his gaze and grinned, her mind racing.

"You want to marry me?" The excitement made her skin tingle. "Me?" *I thought he wanted to break up with me, but no - he wants to marry me? But I'm a terrible girlfriend! I never have dinner on or food in the fridge. I couldn't even train the dog by myself. I bring nothing to the relationship and yet he's proposing. Really, properly proposing to me. Oh my god, he loves me. He genuinely loves me. I can't believe it. Maybe it's some twisted joke and there's a camera crew hiding in the bathroom? No, Marcus would never do that to me. And all this time I was so worried he was up to something. He was finding the right time to propose!* Her sub-concious rambled on inside her head as Marcus spoke.

"Yes, you. It can be you and me, forever." He took the ring from the box and held her left hand. "You still haven't said yes." He laughed, swallowing his doubts. Jennifer giggled and wiggled her wedding ring finger at him. Neither one of them could stop grinning. Jennifer's heart raced in her chest and she looked at her soon-to-be-husband with affection, admiration, lust, desire, love and above all gratitude. She often pondered the idea of her life without Marcus, but it seemed unbelievable. She couldn't imagine a life without both Katherine and Marcus. She needed at least one, if not both of them to fill her heart. *I think Katherine would want me to be happy, to move on from all the pain of her disappearance. Everyone has moved on so why shouldn't I? It's not like I'm forgetting her - I'm just starting a new life with him. She would want me to get married. I just wish she could be at my wedding, that's all. But maybe she will be - maybe she'll hear about it and come back. If she can, that is. No - no sad thoughts, this is a happy moment! I'm getting married to the man of my dreams, of course she would want me to do this. I'm not abandoning her - I'm living my life. It would have been worse for me to stay in that apartment surrounded by memories of her. At least here I can miss her without being overwhelmed. And Marcus has been so understanding about the whole thing from day one. He's always been a dependable man, and he cares for me so much.* Jennifer looked up and realised she still hadn't answered him, and the look on his face told her she should probably speak and make him happy rather than the awkward silence that was currently occurring.

"Yes, Marcus," she grinned at him "I will marry you. I'd love to!" He placed the ring on her finger and hugged her, planting fluttering, light kisses on her face; on her shoulders; her neck. Jennifer laughed as Luca came rushing over to join in the hug, tripping over his big fluffy puppy-paws and sliding the rest of the way until he happily bumped into the sofa and Jennifer's legs. Marcus scratched Luca's ear and the dog barked happily at them. Jennifer pulled the puppy into the hug and laughed as the he wriggled in between them, waiting for them to fuss over him. His tail beat down onto the seat, adding a distorted beat to the atmosphere. Jennifer felt like it was one of those moments in life that ought to have a backing track, but the only noise in the apartment was their voices, the puppy and the dry echo of the iPod playing her "house-cleaning mix" in the kitchen. She weeped with joy as they kissed, embracing each other around the puppy who just observed his human friends as if they were the television: entertaining but ultimately not real.

"And at least you'll have something to do now – you've got a big white wedding to plan." A dry smile crept across Marcus' face, but Jennifer was too busy crying into his shoulder to notice. "No more of this going back to work nonsense, you've got far too much to be getting on with now, darling." He kissed her hair and stroked it until all the fly-away hairs were smooth and back in place. Jennifer just continued to half-wail half-laugh, paying no attention to anything Marcus was saying to her. She was just too happy to listen.

Chapter Thirteen

Jennifer climbed out of the back of the limo, picking up her dress so as not to tread on it, her shoes clicking across the concrete pavement in the dark. Marcus followed behind with her suitcase and lifted her dress from the floor. She opened the building door and struggled through the door. "I can't do this – stop." She put her palm flat on Marcus' tuxedoed chest: "I need to take this train off – Luca will go mental!"

Marcus untied her train and held it, bundled up in his arms. She took her keys from her sleek black clutch bag and unlocked their front door. Luca was nowhere to be seen, but she could hear him barking quietly to himself so she didn't bother looking for him. Marcus followed behind, shutting the door with a backwards kick of his foot. He dropped the things on the sofa and gave an exaggerated sigh. Jennifer stood in the living room in her wedding dress.

"You look very out of place."

"I feel it in this thing!" She picked up the edges of the dress and stared down at them distastefully.

"You look beautiful, though." He smiled, leading her to the bedroom so she could sit down on the bed.

"It's a shame your parents couldn't come to the wedding. It would have been so nice to meet them." Jennifer rubbed her swollen feet and released them from her white high-heeled shoes. Her dress spilled over the edge of her bed, like a giant meringue. She had been complaining all day about how extravagant the wedding had been and that the food was making her feel sick. Marcus thought it might have been her dress; she had said it was too tight, even though it had been altered two weeks before.

Marcus pushed some of her dress aside so he could sit down beside her. His black tuxedo looked shocking next to her white wedding dress, "They were in Jamaica – they couldn't just leave." He fiddled with the trim on the bottom of her gown, twisting it around in his hands.

"I know, I know," she placated him, "But it would still have been nice to actually meet them." She gave a quick smile and stood up. Marcus took hold of her hips and pulled her in front of him, her dress engulfing them. She laughed at the sight: "Why did you insist I have a great big white wedding dress?" She played with the netting that erupted from the waist of her dress.

"So you looked like a princess on our big day. You only get married once, Jen. I wanted it to be special." He mockingly pouted at her.

"It was special, baby." She kissed his forehead and then sat on his lap, surrounding them in the white skirts of her dress. "So, it's my wedding day."

"Our wedding day," he corrected her, tapping her nose with his finger.

"Our wedding day," she repeated. "We're married now; everything is ours." She kissed him again. They glanced around her room and remembered the day she moved in. "So, what are we going to do with this room now we are married? There's no point keeping it as a spare room, no one ever comes to stay." She frowned at the room, boxes in the corner with things she no longer needed, clothes to take to charity, a stereo, a TV. Marcus had taken her shopping when they got engaged: new clothes, new make-up, new everything. They had a Hi-Fi sound system in the living room and a TV bigger than necessary. She didn't need the tatty leftovers from her old life any more; she was starting a new, brighter life with Marcus.

"We could turn it into a library? Or storage?" They both looked at the blank walls of the room. Jennifer had moved into Marcus' room when they got engaged, so she hadn't stayed in her own room for months, but her belongings stayed in her room and she slept in his. They quarrelled over new furniture for their room, what to do once they were married, were they going to move into their first joint home. But they were all empty conversations. The apartment was still Marcus' and he refused to move. Jennifer had learned to agree with him on such matters.

"A library would be nice, or a study – and then you could work from home," she hinted at him, fiddling with her dress. "This itches; can I take it off yet?"

"You've only been wearing it for a few hours."

"A few? I've been wearing it since nine o'clock this morning." Jennifer turned to see the time on the bedside alarm clock. "Twelve hours I've been wearing this thing and it's digging into my hips." She squirmed in her dress. "Please can I take it off?" she pouted at him and he lifted her from his lap, making her stand in front of him.

"Okay, turn around." She did as she was told and turned. He brushed her hair to the front of her shoulder: it was now long, curly and a deep hazelnut brown with a hint of red. She liked dyeing her hair as a surprise to Marcus, but this seemed to be the only colour he had liked so far. Jennifer twirled her hair around her fingers as Marcus unlaced her corset-backed dress. It fell to the floor and she was left standing in her underwear, as white as her dress. She turned to face him again and he had taken off his suit jacket and tie. He hugged her, stroking her hair, her face burrowed into his shoulder. She pulled back and kissed his lips.

"It's our wedding day," she muttered through their kissing.

"I know," he replied, his hands running up and down her back, pushing his body against hers. They kept kissing, blissful in their wedding day glow, until Luca came bounding into the room and pounced playfully on them, pushing them onto the bed. He pawed at Jennifer's exposed chest and nipped at Marcus' shirtsleeves. He was now fully grown, but he seemed to forget he wasn't a puppy any more. He climbed on top of Jennifer and sat on her stomach, his tail wagging, thumping against her leg.

"Get off, Luca. Down boy!" she tried to push him away, but he was too heavy. He just sat there panting and wagging his tail. They laughed, stroking his fur and grinning at each other. Marcus stood up and walked out of the room. Jennifer heard him whistle and Luca crashed out of the room. Marcus rushed back in and locked the door behind him.

"He'll be fine out there for a couple of hours." He said, unbuttoning his shirt.

"Hours?" she lay back on the bed, her arms above her head, stretching out. Marcus threw himself onto the bed, making Jennifer bounce slightly as he hit the mattress. "Am I in your way?" she joked, batting him with her hand. She laughed and closed her eyes, a smile on her face. "I love you," she whispered through her smile.

"I love you too," Marcus replied and kissed her.

Chapter Fourteen

Jennifer flicked through the pages of a glossy magazine, clutching her stomach in pain, with Luca curled up next to her on the sofa. She felt sick again, so she was trying not to move so much. She heard keys in the door and knew it was Marcus coming home.

"Hi," she greeted, without turning around. She listened to him take off his shoes and pad over to the sofa where she sat.

"Hello, babe, you alright? You don't look very well." He stroked her hair gently.

"I feel awful." She started sobbing. Marcus sat down next to her and cradled her.

"What's wrong?"

"I keep feeling sick and dizzy." He pulled back and wiped the tears from her face.

"You've felt like this since the wedding. Is it getting worse?" She nodded at him and threw her head down into his lap, still crying. He grabbed her by the shoulders and picked her up again. "Get up, Jen – I'm taking you to hospital."

She was in so much pain, she couldn't protest. He picked her up and carried her to his car. Marcus lay her down in the back seat and got in the car. Then she fainted, her eyes rolling to the back of her head. Marcus started the engine.

****

"Help, I need a doctor – please!" Marcus carried her through the doors of A & E, nurses rushing to help him. They guided him to a hospital bed in the closest room. He put her down and stepped back.

"Sir – what happened?" The nurses fussed over her, attaching an IV and various other scary-looking tubes.

"She's been feeling sick for weeks now. I came home from a business trip and she was in so much pain. She passed out on the way here." The machines they had hooked to Jennifer started to beep furiously.

"She's crashing – call Dr Morris. Get him out of here!" the nurse yelled orders at the others. A young male nurse pulled Marcus out of the room.

"Sir, just stay here – we are doing everything we can."

"Well, w-what's wrong with her? She just felt sick and then – ."

"Sir, we'll find out, but please just stay out here. I'll come and get you as soon as I can." The male nurse rushed back into the room and closed the blinds, blocking Marcus out.

****

The doctor came out of the room and Marcus stood to attention.

"Well? Is she going to be okay? What happened?"

"Sir, your wife is going to be fine."

"Well. What was that?" He pointed to the room where Jennifer lay sleeping.

"She went into hyperemisis gravidarum - which is basically really severe morning sickness that could actually be very harmful if untreated. It's a good thing you brought her in when you did."

"That's – morning sickness?" He stared at the doctor, confused for a moment.

"She and the foetus are fine now, sir. We've put - "

"Foetus?" Marcus sat down, his hands over his mouth. "So, when she said she was feeling sick, she was having…"

"Morning sickness, yes. Did your wife not know she was pregnant?"

"No, we didn't know, she would have told me. I mean... She does have irregular periods so I suppose we wouldn't have noticed." he huffed. "Jesus, she's having a baby." He looked up at the doctor, sharply. "Is the baby okay?"

"The baby seems to be healthy now; we think her body was just reacting badly to stress, which caused the morning sickness. Both of them are fine now, but she has to be careful not to stress herself, or the baby."

"And why was her morning sickness so bad?"

"It just is with some women, although if your wife didn't know she was pregnant, it probably scared her, causing her to go into shock, which only made the sickness worse. Just make sure she gets a lot of bed rest and takes care of herself." The doctor patted him on the arm and walked away. As he did so, a nurse came out of Jennifer's room.

"Sir, you can see her now. She's a bit drowsy, but she can talk." Marcus stood up and walked over to the door. Jennifer opened her eyes and he rushed to her bedside, sitting on the edge, next to her.

"Marcus?" her voice was cracked and dry.

"Yes, it's me. How you feeling?"

"Thirsty." She half smiled and Marcus picked up the plastic cup of water from the cabinet. He poured the water gently into her mouth and then took the cup away again. He brushed a strand of hair away from her eyes and stared at her. She looked weak and pale, her eyes scanned the room and he guessed that she couldn't remember what had happened.

"Do remember what...?" She shook her head at him. "I came home and you were feeling sick and in pain again, so I carried you out to the car and then you passed out. According to the doctor, you have hyperemisis gravidarum. Which is just severe morning sickness."

"Morning sickness?" she coughed and Marcus gave her some more water. "How – how can I have had that?" Marcus started fiddling with the cup. "What?"

He looked up at her pale face. "Jen, do you need to tell me anything? Anything important that you – maybe you found out whilst I was away?" Her blank expression answered his question and he let out a sigh of relief, mixed with fear. He gripped her hand, "Jen, the doctor said the stress and sickness was caused by the foetus." Her eyes widened.

"I'm not pregnant. There must be some mistake." Marcus shook his head at her. "I can't be..." her voice cracked and she began to cry silently.

Chapter Fifteen

Marcus started buying cribs and baby clothes and toys for their unborn child, long before they were needed. He tried to involve Jennifer, but she spent most of her time either asleep, or staring blankly into the distance. It took weeks for her to come round to the truth: she was having this baby. Abortion wasn't even an option, as they were both against it, but something nagged at Jennifer. She had always wanted a child to love and care for, but she didn't feel right. It wasn't planned, it had been conceived before they were married and now – three months into their marriage, they were planning for a nursery in the room that was supposed to be a study. They had put their lives on hold to prepare for a baby that Jennifer wasn't ready for and the cracks were beginning to show. Whenever Marcus got excited, Jennifer just rolled her eyes and played with the ever-growing dog. She may have accepted that this baby was going to be born, but she didn't like it.

"Do you think we should paint the wall canary yellow or sunset yellow?" Marcus turned around to show the paint chart to Jennifer, but she was fiddling with the bristles of the paintbrush Marcus had chosen. They were standing in the middle of a DIY store and she had nothing to say. "Which one do you prefer, Jen? After all, you're going to be in there most of the time." He smiled, but his remark was returned with a glare.

"Why?" she barked.

"Why what?" He put the chart down on the display stand and walked over to her.

"Why is it going to be me looking after the baby? Why isn't it going to be you?"

"Well, because I have my job and..." Marcus chose his words carefully, but despite his calm tone she was easily aggravated.

"So? I had a job. And I gave it up, for you. I gave everything up for you – my home, my life, my work – even my friends. None of my and Katherine's friends even came to the wedding. They don't care. It was all your work buddies. I'm miserable!" She burst into tears and dropped the brushes, letting them crash to the floor.

This was the first time she had mentioned Katherine since the wedding and Marcus could tell it wasn't going to be the last. "I want my old life back! I don't want this stupid baby!" Marcus recoiled and tried to touch her arm, but she batted him away. "Get away from me! This is all your fault!" she screeched at him and stormed off. He tried to chase after her, but she lost him in the maze of DIY isles. He found her ten minutes later in the baby section, with DIY cribs and wallpaper with ducks swimming across the blue background. He came up to her and hugged her, his arms pulling her close, their stomachs touching as her pregnant belly filled the gap.

"It's okay. I know it's a bit fast, I was in shock too. But, life is a miracle and we have to accept that. Now," he said, pulling back and wiping a tear from her face, "let's go home. We can do this another day." Marcus took her hand and she shuffled behind him obediently.

In the car, she didn't say a word; she just let Marcus waffle on about how great it was going to be when she was a mother and her maternal instincts would kick in, she would see. He was trying to reassure her, but she wasn't listening; his words washing over her as she stared at the motorway. She didn't even notice when they arrived home. She just sat in the car while Marcus carried the shopping inside. He tried to get her out, but she wouldn't move. She stayed in the car until her stomach rumbled and something snapped in her head. She clambered out of the car and slammed the door behind her. When she finally reached the front of the house, she had to knock because she had no keys on her. Marcus opened the door and she could see the worry in his eyes, but she didn't care. She headed straight for the fridge and grabbed the chocolate.

"Honey, I'm just making some dinner, did you want to wait...?" Her glare silenced him and he resumed his food preparations. He chopped the vegetables without a word, while Jennifer sat on the sofa alone, gazing at the TV but ignoring it. She liked the noise and the idea that there was some normality left in the world, even if it wasn't hers. Sometime later, Marcus placed a plate of food on the coffee table in front of her, but she ignored it and let it go cold.

"That's it!" Marcus grabbed the plate and launched it across the room, food flying everywhere – which finally got her attention. "I know you're going through something and I'm sorry but guess what? You can't change anything. You are having this baby – we are having this baby. We are going to raise it and love it; no questions asked. So, whatever this is, just stop!" He stood panting in front of her, his hands on his hips and sweat on his top lip. Jennifer stood up and walked up to him, standing an inch away so their skin almost touched and their tiny unborn baby was between them.

"Took your time," she whispered in his ear and kissed him. She then walked away into her old bedroom. "Aren't you coming?" she called and Marcus rushed into the room, concerned. She lay down in the middle of her bed, wearing only her underwear. Her belly seemed smaller now she was half-naked, but Marcus couldn't ignore its presence.

"But..." He stared at her stomach.

"Ignore it." She didn't look at him, but instead looked to the ceiling, her legs drawn up, so her feet were flat on the bed, but her knees were in the air. Marcus sat at the edge of the bed and leaned over her, being careful not to touch her stomach. For the next hour, they weren't soon-to-be parents who hated each other, they were a young pair of newly-weds enjoying their time together and exploring each other's bodies tenderly.

After that night, Jennifer seemed to be alright for a while, but she had her moments. She was still hesitant to talk about the baby, but focussing on the fact that the birth was months away, helped her. She kept repeating the antics of that night – calling him into the bedroom. But, as it slowly lost its bedroom charm and became a nursery, she became anxious.

"You don't love me any more." It was her favourite phrase to scream at Marcus. As her stomach grew and grew, Marcus became more uncomfortable with her unusually sexual behaviour. He consulted a doctor friend, but they put it down to hormones and told him he should feel lucky that his pregnant wife still wanted to have sex. He tried to fulfil Jennifer's wishes, ignoring the baby when they made love. But as her stomach swelled and the pregnancy progressed, she demanded more intimacy and it became difficult to ignore her baby bump. Marcus even tried touching her stomach on one occasion, but she pushed his hand away and swore at him, demanding he not do it again.

By the time Jennifer was ready to give birth, their marriage was in tatters and they barely spoke. They had gone from the occasional love-making after a huge row, to Jennifer demanding sex at least twice a week. She was emotional, nearly always crying and despite accepting that the baby was on its way, she still wouldn't let anyone mention it. If someone tried to give her a seat on the bus, she screamed at them. When the traffic warden told her she should apply for a parking permit for Mother and Child parking, she assaulted him and got hit with a fine. Marcus couldn't calm her down; the more her pregnancy advanced, the angrier and more depressed she became. The only thing that worked was the sex, because she got to pretend that she wasn't pregnant for an hour or two, which worried him. He could only pray that once the baby was born, she would fall in love with it and regret her behaviour. Until then, it was a guessing game.

The day it happened, Jennifer had been in a department store, looking at all of the beautiful clothes she could wear once she had given birth. She picked up a glittery body-con dress in her size and took it over to the mirror. She held it up against her body and pressed the scratchy material to her skin. She closed her eyes and pretended. Pretended she wasn't a whale in a department store with a dress that wouldn't fit. She was her old self and she was beautiful and happy with her new husband, not the worrying father he had become. Jennifer felt the water rush down her leg and she knew that whether she liked it or not, she was going to have the baby that day.

Twelve hours later and after one of the angriest deliveries the nurses had ever heard, Jennifer was handed a 7lb perfect pink baby girl. She stared down at the whining pink thing that wriggled in her arms and started crying. She begged the young midwife to take the baby away from her and then she fell asleep. The midwives explained to Marcus that childbirth was very stressful and that it was okay for Jennifer to rest, but they made it plain that she needed to bond with the baby, otherwise there might be some issues later.

Marcus spent three days holding that baby, only giving her away to be fed, for which he was so ill-equipped. The midwives whispered about her, wondering if she was fit to be a mother. He complained to the doctor about them and their main midwife was changed for a more sombre elderly woman, who had learned a thing or two about new mothers. The doctor told Marcus that they may need to do some tests on Jennifer, as she wasn't eating properly and he started asking him questions. Had she been behaving strangely? Was she tired a lot? Marcus told the truth and after hours of tests and three more days, they were told they could take their un-named baby home. The doctor told Marcus to keep an eye on Jennifer, as they believed she had postnatal depression, but hopefully after she had spent time with the baby, she would recover. Marcus didn't tell her what was wrong with her and she didn't improve – she just got worse.

They named the baby Katherine, after her best friend, in an attempt that it would cheer Jennifer up, but then every time she heard Marcus use the name, she got angry. She just called the child, Baby.

"I suppose Baby needs feeding?" she would sneer and then reluctantly allow the baby to suckle from her chest. As soon as it was medically advisable, she switched to baby formula and seemed more relaxed for it. One of Jennifer's new obsessions was losing weight and whenever she could, she went to the gym for a couple of hours and by the time Baby Katherine was six months old, Jennifer had lost all of her pregnancy weight and more. When she came back from the gym, she was happier. Not happy, but happier. After she lost all of the weight, she started holding their growing child, which is something she usually avoided at all cost. Marcus thought she was finally getting better.

He returned to work after a month off to help Jennifer care for the new-born, but then he had to go back. Marcus spent his days calling their house phone to check they were okay, but she barely answered. On more than one occasion, he had come home to the baby screaming and Jennifer had music blaring from the Hi-Fi. The first time it happened, he raced into the nursery, dropping his luggage and picked Baby out of the cradle, her head resting on his shoulder as she screamed from hunger. Marcus stormed into the living room and unplugged the Hi-Fi and Jennifer stopped dancing and faced him.

"How long was she screaming?" He swayed gently from side to side, in an attempt to calm the baby down.

"I don't know. I couldn't hear her." She shrugged, kissed him on the cheek and padded into the kitchen. Marcus was left standing with his distressed infant, wondering what had happened to his wife.

Chapter Sixteen

Man got into the habit of bringing Katherine a mug of tea every time he came back to the apartment after she mentioned how her and Jennifer used to drink it all day every day. Katherine refused at first thinking it was drugged, but after a while she accepted the beverage and welcomed it's daily arrival. In the early days, he just bought it from a coffee shop on his way back, but soon he had fitted out the kitchen for all basic cooking needs. He started making her meals and leaving them for her to microwave. Man stopped binding her hands and she learnt to walk a little further with her chained ankles. Despite all this new found freedom, she was still never allowed to leave the confines of the flat. He always locked and chained the door shut from the outside so there was no chance of her escape.

The warm drinks also began to be a pre-apology. Man would give her the drink, talk to her - even have a laugh. But then he would get angry and confused. The first time he hit her, Man started crying. But the second time he seemed to enjoy it. After that, the beatings came as often as the tea did. Katherine thought she could cope with the pain, but then it got worse. She would wake up in the middle of the night and find him on top of her, whispering to himself in the dark. At first, he would just lay there, staring at her, his hands occasionally wondering across her chest. But, just like the beatings - his shyness left and his aggression took over. Katherine wished he would just hit her instead; physical bruises she could handle, but day by day her ego started slipping.

Even though he abused her, they had build a rapport with each other during the day time. He could be kind and civil when he wasn't beating her within an inch of her sanity. Despite months of pain and conversations with Man, Katherine still had no idea who he was or why he was after Jennifer, if that's who he was after. She worried for her best friend out there, not knowing that a madman was looking for her but she knew that whilst she was locked up then he had nowhere to keep Jennifer. This thought soothed her for a little while, until she realised that perhaps Man didn't want to capture Jennifer, but he wanted to kill her instead. And if he did kill her, would he let Katherine go or would she never find out? By the time this had occurred to her, she and Man had been silently living around each other for several weeks, and from the newspapers he brought her, they found out that she was assumed dead and the police search had been stopped. Jennifer had given a beautiful speech about how she missed her best friend and would always be searching for her, but Katherine knew that no matter how hard Jennifer looked for her, they would never be reunited unless she managed to escape the clutches of her prison.

    A few weeks after Katherine read the report about her disappearance, she realised something. She had her phone on her when Man took her. She crawled from her bed, knocking a mug of tea over and letting it shatter on the ground. She made her way over to a box that contained her belongs from her life before her capture. Inside her clutch bag was her smart phone, but the battery was dead. She scrambled to her feet and took the phone into the living room where Man kept some of his belongings and slept sometimes. In a chest of drawers she found a phone charger that matched hers. Tears ran down her face as she saw her phone spring to life. She had no signal and no internet connection but it was a start. Katherine sat by her phone for four hours whilst it charged, and as the sun set the blue light of the phone screen was the only thing brightening the room. Some time later she heard Man start to unlock his many chains on the door and she ripped the charger from the phone and shoved the mobile into her jeans pocket. She tidied the charger away and then wobbled into the kitchen, turning lights on as she went. By the time Man made it through the door, Jennifer was half-way through microwaving her dinner. She greeted him with a nod and then turned her back, watching the plate spin slowly in the microwave. Katherine knew that her only chance to find Jennifer would be to call her somehow. She took her plate out and carried it with two hands in to her room. The heat scalded her hands but she didn't flinch. Her feet shuffled a half-step at a time until she was safely in her bedroom and then she placed the plate on the floor and took the smart phone from her pocket. Katherine unlocked the screen and cried once more as she saw the hundreds of missed phone calls, text messages and voice mails from Jennifer, Joe and her parents. The tears streaked down her face as she scrolled through some of the messages. *Where are you? What happened? Come home! Are you safe? Please answer me Katherine. I miss you.* She wedged the phone between the mattress and the bed post where Man wouldn't find it. She resolved to try and contact Jennifer the next time Man left her alone in the flat and then she would make her escape. It was several weeks before she had a chance to use her phone, Man kept appearing randomly in the day and she didn't want to risk being caught and losing her chance to go home.

****

The minute Man left the flat Katherine grabbed her phone from it's hiding place. She knew he would be gone for a few days, so she would have enough time to call Jennifer, arrange a meeting place and then finally be rid of this terrible ordeal. She swiped the screen and scrolled through her contacts until she found one labelled "Home". She walked the phone around until she managed to find enough signal to make a phone call, and then she tapped the call button on the screen. The phone rang out, so she kept trying. Unbeknown to her, Jennifer had already moved out of their home and moved in with her boyfriend Marcus. She kept redialling the number until finally someone picked up the phone, but it wasn't Jennifer – it was the landlord.

"Hello?"

"Hello – it's Katherine."

"Oh my god."

"Sorry, I know this must be a bit of a shock-"

"You're back from the dead!"

"No, no – I didn't die. I was kidnapped. Listen, I need you to tell Jennifer I called. It's very important you do that, do you understand."

"No, I can't. It's too much for me. This is so weird."

"Sir, please! Where is she?"

"She moved out a few years ago. I almost didn't answer the phone you know – it's been vacant ever since you left. No one wants to live somewhere where a girl died."

"I didn't die, I was taken. Please, can you just tell her I called."

"I can't. But, she did give me her forwarding address for if you ever came back."

"Can I have it?" Katherine frantically looked around for a pen. When she found one, she pulled up her sleeve and wrote the address down that her ex-landlord told her. She hung up the phone and started to pack her things. She took a carrier bag from the kitchen to hold her things, but she realised that all she needed was her phone and what she was wearing. As she put the clothes away, she noticed her dress –

her yellow dress from the night she was taken by Man. Something inside her told her to put it on, because it would help. She stripped off her clothes given to her by her captor and tugged on her old yellow dress. It was too big for her now where she had lost so much weight. Despite Man feeding her, she hadn't seen fruit or vegetables in years. Her hair was matted because he wouldn't let her have a hairbrush and her skin was rough and dry from the cold of her bedroom. Katherine balled her hand around her phone and looked for something heavy. She found a large hammer, covered in unknown greases and oils from years of use, in the living room and used it to start bashing away at the locks on the front door. Hours later, with bleeding hands and grease on her skin from the hammer, she managed to break free. She tugged hard on the door but the chain on the other side stopped it from fully opening. Katherine remembered her ankle chains and smashed herself free, nearly breaking her ankle. She bent slightly and squeezed through the gap in the door. As she did so, the phone dropped from her hand but she was so relived to be free of her prison that she just ran. When Katherine made it outside, the sunlight burnt her retinas for the first time in what felt like years. It warmed her skin in a way she had forgotten. The air whooshed around her bare legs. She found she recognised her location enough to figure out how to make it into town. Katherine didn't know where Jennifer's street was, but she knew that once she got into town, someone would help her and give her directions. She ran down the street, checking for other people around her. She turned right, then left and then ran for ten minutes until she saw the lights of the high street. In her exhaustion, she decided to rest through the night on a bench and then in the morning she would go and find her best friend. Katherine cried herself to sleep and dreamed of a new life and of a fresh start. Tomorrow was the day she finally saw Jennifer's face again and would find out her side of the story and what life had been like for her.

 Days later when Man arrived at the flat, it was Katherine's phone that gave away her escape. He unlocked the door, found the phone lying solitary on the floor and immediately panicked. Man knew exactly where his prisoner would go. It was the end of him.

Chapter Seventeen

Little Katherine squirmed around in the pushchair, passers-by peering in to see the adorable one-year-old in her pretty pink dress and her cute little shoes, but Jennifer sat on the park bench reading a book, ignoring the world – and her daughter. She turned the page, but couldn't concentrate – the child started screaming uncontrollably. She turned the pushchair around and squared up to her infant.

"What? What do you want from me?" Little Katherine continued to scream, so she gave her some juice, which quietened her for a moment. But once the juice was gone, the child carried on screaming.

"Are you hungry? Are you tired? Do you want to go home?" The baby wailed and Jennifer shoved her book in the bottom of the pushchair, picked up her handbag and hurried out of the busy park. People stared at her as she walked with her screaming child, looking to see if Jennifer was going to do anything about it. She had got used to these looks when Marcus started forcing her to take the child outside. He never got the looks, the concerned stares, the worried glances from strangers. He only got smiles, especially from young mothers, thinking he was a single parent. It was driving Jennifer mad, *How is he a better parent than me – he is never here with her. I'm the one stuck with her while she screams,* she thought as she approached the end of her road. The child had stopped screaming and started crying; mumbling to herself and cuddling her teddy bear with the ear bitten off.

Jennifer looked up and saw a homeless woman standing outside her building. At first she thought nothing of it and carried on walking, if somewhat warily. The woman turned towards her, looked at her – squinting as if she had recognised her– and then collapsed. Jennifer ran with the pushchair in front of her until she reached the unconscious woman. She had long matted hair and she was covered in dirt. Jennifer knelt down at the woman's side and turned her over, her hair covered her face, but she didn't wake when she shook her. She put the pushchair, the child sitting happily now inside it, into the apartment and went back outside. The woman was still here. Jennifer looked up and down the street for someone to help her, but there was no one to be seen in the pristine suburban road. She looked down at the thin woman and made a decision. She grabbed her by the arms and dragged her inside. Mumbling apologies as she repeatedly dropped the woman, she finally reached her front door which was ajar. Jennifer could hear the child calling for Luca, who was somewhere in the kitchen, scraping his food bowl against the tiled floor. The woman was small, so Jennifer managed to pick her up and lay her down on the sofa, pushing a changing mat out of the way.

The woman still didn't wake up; she just lay on the sofa: unaware of what was going on around her. Little Katherine crawled around the floor, occasionally tugging at the woman's hair, to see if she would like a teddy bear. Luca sat growling at her until he grew bored and found his favourite chew toy. Jennifer fussed, bringing her food and water for when she woke up. She tried talking to her, shaking her, yelling at her, but the woman did not wake. The room was nearly dark before Jennifer realised how much time had passed, so she begrudgingly moved from her observation seat and turned on the lights. She fed the child and the dog and resumed her watching position. It was the sound of Jennifer's mobile ringing that finally woke the woman up. Jennifer checked the caller ID and answered the phone.

"Hey, babe." She watched as the woman started to stir.

"Wow, you sound better. Is everything okay?" Marcus' tinny phone voice echoed.

"Yes, yeah, no every thing's fine. We've just had a good day that's all. Actually, I was wondering – I know you're supposed to be coming home tonight..." *I need to stall him, he will go crazy if he sees some homeless woman on our sofa*, she thought.

"Yeah?" He replied, concerned.

"Do you mind... not?" she hesitated, biting her lip, looking at the woman as she opened her eyes.

"Huh?"

"I just want to spend some time with her by myself, you know: mother-daughter bonding." Jennifer put her finger to her lips and her expression begged the woman to stay silent.

"Oh. Well, say no more – I'll come back tomorrow evening instead. Does that sound okay?"

"Yes, perfect. Bye. I love you, Marcus." The woman's eyes widened at the sound of his name.

"I love you too. And babe?" Jennifer wasn't listening any more. "I'm so glad you're feeling better. Maybe we can start being a real family now." And with that, she hung up the phone.

The woman started coughing, so she handed her the glass of water from the table.

"Thank you." Strange, Jennifer thought, she doesn't sound like a homeless person. In fact, she's not even that dirty... it's only her clothes.

"That's alright. Um, do you mind if I ask you a question?" Jennifer mumbled. What am I doing?

"Go for it."

"Why were you outside my house? Do you know someone in the building?" she enquired.

"Yes, two people actually. One is a dear friend I haven't seen in a long time..." The woman's voice trailed off and she started sobbing. "I'm so sorry." Jennifer, confused, put her hand on the woman's shoulder and looked at her clothes. She noticed the woman had on a tattered man's jumper over what looked like a dress.

"Here, why don't I get you some new clothes? I'm sure I have something that would fit." Jennifer walked off and went into the bedroom. She grabbed a t-shirt and some leggings and then came back into the living room. "The bathroom is over there - you can shower and stuff. Maybe you'll feel better." The woman stood and took off the man's jumper, handing it to Jennifer. The dress looked like it used to be tight, but over the years where the woman had lost weight, it hung off of her. She pulled it over her head and handed it to Jennifer, who stood staring at the woman's frail frame.

The woman took the new clothes and went into the bathroom. Jennifer's head spun, so she went to the kitchen for water. She turned on the tap, putting the clothes on the kitchen worktop for a moment. Once she had a glass of water, she leant with her hip touching the kitchen surface, drinking. Her hands shook and she spilt some water on the dress. As she touched the material to wipe the water away, the dirt lifted from the dress and she realised it was yellow. Jennifer thought nothing of it and threw the clothes away. She finished her drink and went into the bedroom to find some more clothes for the woman to take away with her. If she is homeless, or in trouble, I don't want her freezing to death. She found an old rucksack and stuffed the clothes inside. She picked it up and walked into the living room. As she did so, the woman emerged from the bathroom, clean and dressed. She had obviously found scissors in the bathroom, because she had shorn her hair off into an uneven bob which she was now towel-drying. *That's no homeless woman,* she thought. Jennifer dropped the rucksack on the floor and stared at the woman.

"Do you recognise me now?" The woman continued to dry her hair, hope and sarcasm tinting the fear in her voice.

"Yes." Jennifer gasped and ran other to the woman, drawing her into a bear hug. They stood embracing, swaying slightly as the emotion swept other the both of them. They sobbed into each other's shoulders.

"I never thought I would see you again," the woman cried.

"I thought you were dead," Jennifer answered and pulled back in reaction to her own sentence. "I thought you were dead!" she repeated angrily. "Where the hell were you?"

"You aren't going to like the answer. Here," the woman gestured, "you'd better sit down, Jen." Jennifer did as she was told and Little Katherine came crawling over to the two women, wondering what all the fuss was about. "Oh, who is this?" the woman pinched the little girl's cheeks.

"I called her Katherine." The other woman stopped what she was doing and looked up, with tears in her eyes.

"You named your daughter after me?" Katherine asked.

END OF PART 1

PART TWO

Chapter Eighteen

Jennifer and Katherine sat on the sofa drinking tea, letting the steam heat their faces. Little Katherine sat on Katherine's lap, tugging at her hair and mumbling. Jennifer finished speaking.

"... so then I got pregnant and have basically spent the last two years miserable and not knowing what to do with her. At one point, I even considered leaving her with Marcus and moving away." She gazed down at her daughter and saw her for the first time. She looked her child in the eyes, cradled in the arms of her best friend and finally felt that pang of maternal instinct she had been waiting for. She took the child and smelled her hair. The child stopped mumbling and nestled into her mother's shoulder and fell asleep. It was the first time Jennifer had ever hugged her daughter and in that moment, she wondered why she had never done it before.

"Marcus would never have let you do that, he's too controlling." The sound of Katherine speaking drew her out of her epiphany.

"He isn't controlling..." Jennifer frowned and kissed Little Katherine's head.

"Not of you, I guess not..." Katherine's voice trailed off and she turned her attention to her tea. Jennifer was barely listening as she admired her daughter's beautiful blue eyes.

"Katherine, are you going to tell me where you've been? Why did you leave?"

"I didn't leave. I've been in Canterbury this entire time."

"What?" Jennifer's voice cracked a little.

"I didn't vanish by choice, you know. I was taken..."

"By who? The police thought it was Joe –"

"How is he?" Katherine interrupted, the desperation sang in her voice, in her eyes.

"I don't know: we fell out just before I moved in with Marcus." Jennifer stroked Little Katherine's back as she stood. She walked into the nursery and placed the child gently down in the crib, drawing the blankets up and over her small body. She bent down and kissed her daughter again, before walking out and shutting the door. "He was a suspect, you know," Jennifer continued and then stopped when she saw Katherine's face. "It wasn't Joe, was it?"

"God, no." Katherine shook her head and patted the sofa seat next to her. Jennifer sat down and took Katherine's hands.

"Tell me who did this. We can tell the police, we can –" Jennifer stopped and shuddered.

"What?"

"Your parents think, I thought...we all thought you were dead. When Joe was the only suspect, the locals started hounding him. I don't even know where he lives." She breathed out. "We need to go to the police."

"It's not that simple."

"Why not?"

"My kidnapper has a family and I don't know if I could ruin their lives just for my own sake."

"Who cares? They should know what he is like, what he did... What did he do?" She turned more towards her best friend.

"He kept me in a flat on the other side of town. He would come and visit me every week with food, magazines and things like that. Then after a while he started beating me, raping me... He just liked to watch me suffer. I felt like a caged pet or something – doing tricks for his amusement." Katherine shuddered.

"How did his wife not notice he was going away for so long?" she enquired.

"He told her he was going away for business trips." Katherine looked Jennifer in the eyes, waiting.

"Ridiculous. I mean, the nerve of some people – who does he think he is, keeping you prisoner. Did he even tell you why he took you?"

"Yes. He told me on day one."

"Well?" she asked, surprised.

"He said he 'took the wrong girl.'" Katherine waited again and watched as Jennifer's life crumbled from underneath her, struggling to breathe as she sobbed.

"But –" Katherine held her hands, stroking them with her thumbs, in a failed attempt to comfort her. "I was... I was with you. Did – did he mean me?"

Katherine nodded and watched as her best friend broke down. "Who is he? Tell me!" she screamed.

"You don't want to know, Jen."

"He tortured you for years! He stole you out of a nightclub – no one even saw you leave. Who is he? What if he's done this before?"

"He hasn't done it before." Katherine responded calmly.

"Well, how do you know – he could have lied. Kidnappers are hardly trustworthy."

"Neither are husbands." Katherine's eyes bore into Jennifer, willing her to understand her coded references.

"What do husbands have to do with it?"

"You have a husband."

"So?"

"And I have a kidnapper."

"What does that have to do with it?"

"Oh, Jen – everything. Two sides of one coin." Jennifer's hand clasped to her mouth as it sunk in.

My husband, Marcus. He did that, he did all of this. And it was meant for me. Katherine wasn't even... oh my God. "... I married him! We have a daughter and he's had you locked up for the whole time?" She struggled, crying and breathing heavily, tears streaming down her face, her nails digging into her arms as she hugged herself, rocking forwards and backwards. She sat for a few minutes, thinking about her life with Marcus. *Why didn't I notice any of this? He was always so caring... I felt like the bad guy – not him. I was worried our marriage was falling apart because of –* she stopped thinking and stood up, rushing into the nursery. Katherine followed.

"What are you doing?" Katherine stood in the doorway as Jennifer packed up her daughter's things.

"We need to leave, now. Marcus is coming home tomorrow from a business trip. And if he's on a business trip then he's –" She didn't stop packing.

"– Going to go to see me. But I'm not there," Katherine finished. "Oh my god, he's going to know. He will know this is where I came."

"How did you even know I was here?"

"Our old landlord - I had to use Marcus' charger on my phone..." They sat silently looking at each other until they burst into laughter, shaking through the horror, but still managing to see the funny side. They both knew they had to laugh, because admitting the danger of the situation they were in might just drive them insane.

Chapter Nineteen

"We need to leave, how much money can you get together by tonight?" Katherine didn't pause long enough for Jennifer to answer. "We can take the baby and leave the country or go somewhere he might never find us. Then we can figure out what to do."

"What are you going to do in the meantime?"

"Get some sleep in a B and B or something." Jennifer walked over to her handbag and pulled out her purse.

"Here," she said, handed Katherine some cash. "Take this – keep out of sight. Call me when you can." She jotted her number on the back of an old receipt. "We should probably pack some food and stuff. How much do you think you can manage to carry into town?" The women made up a large holdall of provisions for both of them and Little Katherine, including some clothes and food – just in case Jennifer didn't have a chance to pack.

When it was time for Katherine to leave, they hugged – crying in the doorway.

"You better go, just in case. Don't forget to call me when you're settled and let me know where you are." They hugged one last time and Katherine walked away laden with the bags, preparing to start a life on the run.

Jennifer packed her and Little Katherine's bags and hid them in the nursery wardrobe. Then, she took her now happy baby girl and went into town. As she hurried to the bank, her mobile rang.

"It's me. I'm at the B and B on the corner by the West Gate Towers, Room 4. Where are you?"

"I'm getting money and then I'm going to bring Katherine and the bags to you."

"Why?"

"Because I need to do something before I leave." She hung up the phone and entered the bank. As she approached the cashier, she placed a fake smile on her face.

"Hello, I was wondering if you could help me."

"Of course, what can I do for you today?" asked the alarmingly orange-skinned cashier.

"I need to take out all of my money. Could you tell me how much that is?" She handed over her card.

"In your personal account or joint?" the woman smiled at her.

"Personal, please."

"£96,345, ma'am," she stated.

"Sorry?"

"£96,345," she repeated, speaking clearly.

"Uh, right. That sounds like a lot, are you sure?" Jennifer glanced over her shoulder.

"Yes, ma'am. £90,000 was transferred into your account last week."

"Could you tell me by whom?"

"It doesn't say ma'am. How much would you like to take?" The woman seemed to be getting worried.

"How much can I take out in one day?"

"£10,000, ma'am."

"That will do. Thanks."

"I will have to get my manager to authorise it, ma'am," she warned.

"No problem. I'll wait here." Jennifer tried to stay calm and had to clasp her hands together in order for them to stop shaking. After a minute or two, the cashier appeared with a plump forty-something man in a grey suit.

"Everything alright ma'am?"

"Yes, thank you. I would like to withdraw £10,000 from my account please."

"May I ask why?"

"I'm moving abroad."

"It isn't wise to carry cash of this amount on your person –."

"Oh no, I have to give the money to my partner to pay for my half of the apartment. He doesn't trust online banking so he'd rather do it in person." Jennifer kept her voice steady and her head held high.

"Very well," the manager allowed, handing her a form, "if you could just sign here and then we will get you the money." Jennifer filled out the form and took her money. The security guard offered to walk her to her car, but she declined. She stuffed the money envelope into her handbag and headed home. As she neared her apartment, her phone rang. She saw the caller ID and started to panic.

"Hi babe, I was wondering when I could come back? Only I'm getting a bit bored in the hotel by myself. I know you wanted to spend some time with Katherine, but –."

"Well I'm just getting home actually, we went to the park and we had some lunch. I got some bits for dinner, so if you could be home for 6pm tonight, that would be lovely." She kept her cool and Marcus fell for it.

"Sounds great. Babe, I am so happy you've come around to this. You wait; it's going to be amazing." She hung up the phone and let the breath escape. She didn't realise she had been holding her breath until then. Jennifer sped up and by the time she got through the front door, she was crying. Little Katherine mumbled at her.

"No, sweetie. You have to stay in the pushchair, we are going again. You're going to stay with Auntie Katherine whilst Mommy figures out what to do." Jennifer grabbed the bags and headed back out of the door.

When she reached the B and B, the receptionist pointed her in the right direction and she reached upstairs in the elevator. Little Katherine wobbled her teddy bear around in front of her own face, seemingly happy and unaware of the danger they were in. The doors pinged open and Jennifer turned left out of the elevator, to find door No 4. She found it after a few seconds and knocked gently. Katherine opened the door and smiled, allowing Jennifer to wheel the pushchair and child inside, bags hanging from each shoulder.

"I packed as much as I could. Hopefully I have time to grab some more before I leave." She dropped the bags on the floor. "Are you two going to be okay for a few hours?" Jennifer blew a kiss to her daughter and waved goodbye.

"Where are you going?"

"He called me; he's going to be home at six. I need to be there. If he is as dangerous as you say he is, he won't just let me disappear – he'll know something is up. I'm just going to say that your parents came to visit and the baby is with them. I'll say I'm going to stay with them for a few days with her and then I'll make something up. Remember to give them the address of the flat so they can get a search warrant, there should be enough evidence there to put him away for life." Jennifer took her handbag off the pushchair and opened the door.

"It's not safe" Katherine protested, but nothing she could say would change Jennifer's mind.

"I need to go. He's my husband. Love you." She hugged Katherine and then walked back out the door.

****

Jennifer was standing in the kitchen chopping mushrooms when Marcus came home. As the front door clicked open, she took a deep breath and put on her best smile. She had showered and changed since coming home, wearing a tight black dress and heels. It was the first time she had worn make-up in months. She heard Marcus come up behind her and tried not to recoil in horror as he snaked his arms around her waist.

"Hello, beautiful."

"Hi." She turned around and kissed her husband, gently moving him out of the way to put a dish in the sink.

"Where's the baby?"

"She's with Katherine's parents. I saw them in town today and they asked if they could baby sit for the night." She smiled, popping a cherry tomato in Marcus' mouth. "So it's just me and you tonight."

"I don't know how I feel about leaving her with strangers."

"They aren't strangers; they are my dead best friend's parents. I wasn't going to say no, especially after how I have been lately." She lowered her gaze, pretending to feel guilty. Marcus cupped her face.

"I'm sorry – it was a great idea. Thank you." He gently kissed her lips. "I'm going to go have a shower and then we can have dinner. Does that sound about right?"

"Yeah – make it a quick one though, I don't want my sauce burning," she warned and he left her alone in the kitchen holding a large knife. Jennifer picked up her phone from the kitchen counter and called the B and B.

"Room 4 please." She waited to be connected. "Hello?"

"Is everything okay?"

"I need you to listen carefully, because I can't repeat this: call the police. Tell them the truth, but don't tell them where I am. Ask them to meet you at the B and B and I will be there tonight. I've got to go – he's only in the shower. Goodbye." She hung up the phone and returned to her cooking, stirring the deep red sauce and picturing all of the unimaginable things that Katherine must have been through over the past four years. Jennifer dished up the dinner and placed it on the dining room table, lighting some candles and playing romantic music in the background. Marcus emerged ten minutes later wearing jeans and a light blue shirt.

"Oh well, doesn't this look nice?" he gestured to the table. "Thank you, sweetie." Jennifer tottered over to him in her heels and kissed his cheek.

"It's my way of saying sorry." They sat down to eat. "So how was your trip?"

"Dull, got to play some golf though, so that was nice." Jennifer watched her husband lie through his teeth. *Does he even have a job? Katherine has said it was only once a week that he came to the apartment – so where was he the rest of the time? And where did all that money come from?* She smiled, listening to Marcus talk about a business meeting he had during the week. They finished their meal and Jennifer washed up the dishes.

"So, what's for dessert?" Marcus leaned in the kitchen doorway and grinned at her. Jennifer led him to the bedroom and made love to her husband for the last time. When she was sure he was asleep, she crept out of bed and got dressed. As she went to leave the bedroom, Marcus stirred.

"Where are you going?"

"Apparently Katherine won't go to sleep without me, I'm just going to see her and tuck her in. I won't be long, go back to sleep." She waved goodbye and shut the door behind her. Jennifer walked into the nursery, grabbed the bag she had hidden earlier and left the apartment. She ran to the taxi rank and climbed into a cab. Jennifer cried for the entire journey.

When she reached the B and B, she could see a police car parked up outside. She paid the taxi driver and got out, remembering her bag. The receptionist recognised her and let her walk passed. When Jennifer knocked on the door of No 4, a tall policeman answered. As she walked into the room, she saw a man she recognised.

"Jennifer, I believe we've met before – DI Johnson."

"Yes, sorry – hello. Thank you for coming."

"Not at all, I requested I be the one to take the call out. When I heard you were involved, I knew something was going on. Miss Luca has been telling us her version of things. Would you mind filling in some blanks?"

"Of course."

"When did you meet the suspect?"

"I met Marcus a couple of weeks before Kat went missing."

"And when did you see him after?"

"A couple of weeks, I think – maybe a month."

"And when did you move in with the suspect?"

"A few months after Katherine went missing."

Jennifer sat and told DI Johnson her side of the story, only interrupted occasionally by the static noise of the accompanying officers' radios, telling them of crimes being committed in the area. *Shouldn't they answer those calls? People should be getting hurt*, she thought as she told her tale.

When she finished, an officer handed her a tissue. She didn't realise she was crying. "I'm fine," she lied and fidgeted in her seat.

The room felt cramped, mostly due to the extra bodies and the pram in the corner, but more so because she felt trapped. On her way to the B and B, she had felt liberated, but now she felt as if she were betraying her husband. But she only had to glance at Katherine's frail frame to remind her that her husband was a monster.

The police confirmed the dates the two women had given them with the police report and confined themselves in the corner. Jennifer moved over to the bed on the left side of the room, where Katherine sat day-dreaming.

"Are you alright?"

"Yeah, it's just strange, you know."

"Why is it strange?"

"Well, I spent all of this time escaping, but now I'm just trapped in another room with people staring at me. It doesn't feel any different."

"Well, when this is over, you can get a good night's sleep and then we can work from there. This won't be easy, so I want you to know that I am with you every step of the way."

"Jen, I need to ask you something."

"Go for it."

"Why did you call her Katherine?" She nodded towards the pram.

Jennifer took a deep breath and put her hands on her knees. "Because I knew you weren't dead. I don't know how, but I just knew. When I had her, I thought that if I called her Katherine, you might come back to me and things would be the way they used to be."

Katherine stared at her best friend. "Things will never be the same. You know that, right?"

"Yeah, I know."

"But, we can start again." Katherine smiled, placing her bony hand on her friend's shoulder.

"A fresh start: we can move to the country." Jennifer picked a piece of fluff from her leg.

"Can we have sheep?" Katherine joked.

"We can have sheep. Maybe even a duck pond," she grinned.

"It would be nice to have a garden – I've missed the feel of grass under my feet."

"Then we will have grass and lots of it. I wouldn't dream of buying an apartment. Not after..." Jennifer's voice trailed off. "Sorry – I shouldn't bring it up."

"Why not? It happened. It was four years of my life – you can't not bring it up." Jennifer shrugged in response. "Jen, it's okay."

"Yeah, but it's not – is it? Marcus, he – he kidnapped you and then he married me."

"From what you told the cops, I'm not the only one that was a prisoner."

"What are you on about?"

"You gave up your job, Jen. You loved it there. You had no friends; you only got married for security. Any woman would have done it."

"What?"

"You married him because you were lonely and frightened. Do you really think our friends didn't try to contact you over all of those years? He must have blocked their numbers or something. Maybe he threatened them. You don't know. In fact, have you even bumped into a single one of them since you met him?"

"Uh, well – I don't... no." Jennifer put her head in her hands and cried. "Was everything about my life a lie? Surely some of it was true?"

"He loved you. That was true." Jennifer looked up.

"I don't think I loved him. Ever. He was just so... comforting. He gave me what I wanted when I wanted it. When I was lonely the first time, he bought me a dog. When I was angry with him because he was never there, he married me. Once we were married, we had a baby."

"He was trying to make a life with you. Just on a time scale. What I don't get is how you didn't notice he was gone for so long?"

"Because I didn't care. Whenever he was away, I could pretend I was me, me with you and our old life. Sure at the start, I was as involved as any woman would have been. But after we got married, I just felt more alone than ever." She sobbed and Katherine rubbed her back gently, her palm flat on her back. "I wanted you to be there on my wedding day."

"I know, I know." she soothed. "But we are starting again. You can get a divorce; we can get a new house, me, you and the baby."

The DI walked back over. "Ladies, I am going to station these two officers to keep an eye on you tonight, just in case Marcus figures out where you are. Tomorrow, they will bring you down to the station to take your official statements. For now, get some rest." He shook their hands, grasping them firmly and then let himself out of the room. The officers followed, but stood guard outside the door. The static from their radios buzzing in the corridor.

****

In the morning, the officers drove the two women and the baby to the police station. Little Katherine sat on Jennifer's lap, squirming as the car sped over bumps. No more than ten minutes later, they were sat in DI Johnson's office and Little Katherine was crawling around his floor. She found a paper clip and started to grab at it. Katherine picked her up and held her firmly on her lap.

"You mustn't do that, picking things up. Its naughty." The child giggled, mumbling at Katherine in her own language, drool running down her chin. Katherine wiped it away with her thumb and returned her attention to the DI. As he started to speak, a ringing erupted from Jennifer's bag.

"That's my mobile." She checked the caller ID. "What do I do, it's Marcus?" She started to panic.

"Tell him you'll be home soon, you've just gone for breakfast," stated DI Johnson, watching her carefully.

Jennifer answered the phone and did as she was told. "Hey babe." Her voice smiled but her face was pale and worried.

"Where are you? I woke up and you were gone. Is everything all right?" his voice echoed through the phone and she could hear him turning on the shower.

"Yes, no problem. I fell asleep on their sofa, so we're going to go for breakfast and then I'll be home." Jennifer couldn't focus her gaze on anything, the room spun around her and she couldn't catch her breath.

"Are you okay?" Marcus' voice sounded troubled in her ear.

"I feel great. Honestly, the best I have in ages. Love you." she lied.

"Love you." He hung up the phone and Jennifer put the phone on the desk. "Please don't make me do that again." She picked the phone up after a second and held it out to DI Johnson.

"You won't have to." He took the phone from her and sealed it in an evidence bag. "We've got officers on the way to your home now. He will be taken into custody – then we go from there. I just need you two to make your official statements and then we can begin proceedings." He waved to an officer outside the door, who entered and nodded his head in greeting.

"Officer Michaels will take your statement Jennifer and I will be taking Katherine's." Jennifer stood up and took the baby from Katherine. She followed the officer out of the room and down a dark grey corridor. The lights were bright to her tired eyes.

"Can I take my daughter with me?" she asked Officer Michaels, jiggling the child up and down on her hip. The officer turned and stopped at the sound of her voice.

"She'll have to wait outside the interview room I'm afraid, but Officer Raine will keep an eye on her." He glanced over her shoulder and nodded. A female officer approached out of nowhere and smiled at Jennifer.

"She'll be okay with me for a while ma'am, not to worry. I've five children myself." She spoke with a soft Birmingham accent that both soothed and worried Jennifer. She cautiously handed her child over to the curvy woman and then followed Officer Michaels, looking briefly over her shoulder to see Little Katherine tugging at the woman's yellow curly hair.

The officer led her into INTERVIEW ONE and gestured to the seat on the left. The room had a black metal table and a chair either side. There was a recording machine at the far end of the table, with the microphone pointing towards Jennifer's chair. She sat where she was told and looked around. There was nothing on the walls, no posters, no windows. There was a long bar light above their heads with the same intensity as the ones in the corridor.

"I feel like I'm about to be interrogated, not interviewed." She laughed shakily and the officer smiled, sitting in his seat.

"Okay Jennifer, I am going to turn this machine on and ask you some questions. You need to be honest with you answers and know that if you lie to us, you will be charged with with-holding information."

"Yes, uh – okay." She wasn't sure how to respond to his clipped voice. Her hands shook and her foot tapped sub-consciously on the concrete floor. Jennifer shivered, but she wasn't sure if it was from the metallic chill of the room, or the fear in her heart. Despite being innocent in the matter, she felt responsible for it all.

"Jennifer, in your own words: explain the event of Katherine's disappearance." He interrogated her for an hour before she was allowed to leave the interview room. She walked out shaken up and feeling dizzy. She had been honest and true to her account, but part of her felt she had covered for Marcus.

"Was he ever violent towards you?"

"No. If anything, I was the abusive one in the marriage."

"Why is that?"

"I had postnatal depression, uh and I became a bit… angry."

"Did you ever attack your husband?"

"Only verbally." It was the first time Jennifer had admitted her problem to a stranger and despite the relief, she was also aware of the shame she felt. Not only for the way she had treated her seemingly loving husband, but the way she had treated her daughter. Her own flesh and blood and she had acted as if she were a random child, a pest in her otherwise fake-beautiful life. Sitting in that box room, she realised that in the chaos that had become her life, her child was the only honest and unblemished beauty left. Her husband was a liar, her friends had been bribed and her best friend was crazed by the torture and isolation she had suffered.

She was escorted from INTERVIEW ONE to Officer Raine's cubicle in the office space. Little Katherine was crawling across the metre of carpeted floor, chasing a wind-up mouse. The female officer watched her with glee in her eyes and a genuine smile on her lips. Her maternal instincts overrode her professionalism, though not in a manner that anyone could deem inappropriate. Jennifer, for the first time, felt a sense of pride for her daughter. Even though she had treated her cruelly by ignoring her, she had still become a perfect little human being and Jennifer loved her for it. Little Katherine was a joyful child in absence of a joyful childhood thus far and Jennifer made a promise to herself that her daughter would never know what her father had done and that she would know only happiness in her life.

Jennifer's heart ached as she looked at her chubby baby and she scooped her up in her arms, smelling her hair and cradling the giggling child back and forth. Little Katherine squirmed in her arms, so she put her on the floor, holding the child's arms above her head. As she did so, the child stood tall and took a brave, if wobbly step forward. The child pulled away from her mother's hands and toddled away towards the waste paper bin, chasing the toy mouse. She retrieved it and presented it proudly to Jennifer. Jennifer stood shocked and heartbroken. She picked up her little girl and kissed her on the cheeks, the nose, pecking kisses all over her angelic face. The child squirmed again and Jennifer let her toddle around the cubicle, being watched proudly by the two women.

Later that day

After leaving the police station and being told they couldn't leave town as they may be needed for more questioning, the women and the toddler returned to their room and awaited further instructions. An officer continued to guard them, in case Marcus showed up. They ordered a pizza and turned on the TV.

"Why haven't they arrested him yet?" enquired Katherine, nibbling on a pizza crust, her legs crossed underneath her. She perched nervously at the end of the bed.

"They need to check over our statements first." She took a bite from the pizza slice in her hand and winced when she realised it was still hot, blowing on the slice in a failed attempt to cool the hot dough. "If he's trying to call me, it won't be long until he realises something has happened. He will come looking for me. And, if he's as twisted as you say he is" – she paused, shifting in her seat and taking another bite of her pizza – "then it won't take him much longer to figure out exactly what happened." As she spoke, she heard the crackle of the officer's radio and his mumbled voice urgently responding. She moved the pizza box onto the floor space between the beds.

The officer gave a rapid knock at the door and entered. "Good news." He stood a little taller, squaring his shoulders. He placed his radio back onto his jacket. "Marcus has been arrested and is now in custody. They'll question him, hopefully get a full confession and then go from there." The women breathed a sigh of relief simultaneously and hugged each other.

"What if you don't get a full confession?" Jennifer worried.

"We have enough evidence to prove his guilt. I wouldn't worry about it if I were you, ladies."

Little Katherine sat unaware on the floor, absorbed in a cooking programme, tugging at her clothes, drool escaping her mouth.

"I'm afraid I'll have to stay here with you until he's been moved to a local prison, but after that you should be fine." He backed out of the room and left them alone to enjoy the moment. Jennifer called Little Katherine over and bundled her into the embrace, squeezing tightly, her tears of joy wetting the child's hair. They sat like that for some time, just enjoying the safety of the hug: knowing that despite the cruelty they had faced, they would never be in danger again. They could move on and have new lives – with each other.

Katherine pulled out of the embrace first. "Where are we going to go? We have nowhere to go." She shuffled back a little to give Jennifer room to breathe.

"We could stay with your parents? Do they even know you're alive?" Jennifer queried, sitting a little straighter and rubbing her eyes.

"Yes, the police phoned them to let them know. Apparently, they were still trying to find my body." Her voice cracked towards the end of the sentence and she rested her head on Jennifer's shoulder. "All those years, they didn't give up – even though the police did. They still hoped I was still alive, like you." She mumbled into Jennifer's neck, crying gently.

"It's okay. It's going to be okay, hunny." Jennifer soothed her, repeating herself over and over, rubbing her back, whilst still holding onto her daughter, who was slowly drifting off to sleep. "Get some sleep, you two. Then tomorrow we can start our new lives, together." On cue, the two Katherine's drifted off, their bodies relaxed and Jennifer laid them both down on the beds. Jennifer got up from the bed and moved away from them. She sat on the floor, staring blankly at the television, watching the world carry on without her. She brought her knees up to her chest and rested her chin on top of them, the cold material of her jeans shocked her, but she stayed sat on the floor, not moving an inch. Jennifer didn't really like wearing jeans, but she didn't know whether it was because Marcus didn't like them, or she didn't.

Jennifer listened to the police radio through the door, finding comfort in it, knowing she wasn't alone. She was still awake when the officers switched over for the end of the shift. She heard their banter and their normality. She envied the way they coped with these situations: they weren't upset or confused – they knew how to behave and what to do. Jennifer wanted that emotional reserve to fall back on and to make her brave. Because now not only did she have a daughter to protect from the world, but she also had Katherine, who had been removed and detached from all things real for four years. Her adjustment to real life was going to be a challenge for all of them.

Chapter Twenty

Katherine, Jennifer and the baby went to stay with Katherine's parents for a while, but upon arrival they noticed a black car in the driveway. A big flashy 4 X 4 Land Rover with cream leather seats and several shopping bags in the back.

"Who the hell is that?" Katherine frowned as she climbed out of the taxi. They had just got the train and it had been raining, so they called a cab.

"Is it not your Dad's?" Jennifer paid the cab driver and he helped her get their luggage and the pushchair from the boot of the taxi.

"No way, Dad would never drive something that big." They walked past the 4 X 4, glaring at it and went to the front door. Jennifer had her daughter on her hip, a bag over her shoulder and she was dragging suitcases behind her. Katherine's parents rushed out to help them with their things, the rain getting heavier by the minute.

The moment they were inside, Katherine's parents mobbed her, kissing and hugging her, crying. But she just stood there. She smiled and received the hugs, but she looked out of place in her parents house. She was thin and pale, where they were tanned and chubby with old age. She hugged herself, her hands on her elbows as they guided them into the living room, where Jennifer noticed a briefcase neatly stood on the floor at the edge of the sofa. She coughed and nodded to it, catching Katherine's attention. Katherine pulled away from her parents' grasp.

"Who is here? Other than us?" she looked around the room, warily.

"Katherine –" Their expressions were dark and serious, tears still escaping their eyes.

"Who is here?" she yelled, her paranoia getting the better of her. Both Katherine and Jennifer thought the same thing, so were surprised when a man walked out of the kitchen in a blue suit drinking a cup of tea. Her parents smiled brightly, her father hugging her mother's shoulders with his left arm.

"Joe?" Katherine's voice cracked and she ran over to him, giving him just enough time to put the mug down on the nest of tables. She wrapped her arms around his neck and buried her face into his shoulder. "I never thought I would see you again," she bawled. Her tears dampened his blue suit, but he didn't care. Joe held her close, as if he never wanted to let her go again. They stood hugging and crying for a moment, the rest of the room watching – except Little Katherine, who had found a cat to annoy. The cat tried to bat the infant away, but her tiny pink hands grabbed its fur, roughly stroking it. The cat gave up and sat on top of the child's legs, letting Little Katherine tangle her long black fur.

Katherine, still hugging Joe, turned to face everyone else.

"It's going to be okay now, isn't it?" she beamed, closing her eyes and resting her head against his shoulder. She felt warm inside, as if her heart was trying to burst out of her chest; she was happy in that moment.

****

"So, how did you know she was back?" Jennifer asked, plaiting Little Katherine's hair. The living room was lit only by the fire and a lamp. It was warm and drowsy.

"Her parents phoned me, but I've been involved in the case for some time now." Joe had taken his suit jacket off and had stretched his arm against the back of the black leather sofa. Katherine was asleep between them, her head in his lap, breathing quietly like a child. Her parents had gone upstairs to give the three of them a chance to catch up, but the excitement of seeing Joe again had exhausted her and Katherine had fallen asleep by 8pm. Joe and Jennifer were left alone and very much awake.

"What happened... after...?" Jennifer's voice trailed off. She felt guilty for the way she had treated Joe. He had known there was something wrong about Marcus, but her emotions had clouded her judgement and now four years later – here they were.

"I left town, moved to Scotland for a year and built up a business."

"Oh, what kind of business?" she absent-mindedly asked, finishing Little Katherine's plait and picking the child up.

"I buy and sell companies." Jennifer placed Little Katherine in her pushchair and kissed her goodnight. She fell straight to sleep.

"Sounds dull, is there a lot of money in that kind of thing?"

"Quite a bit, yeah." Joe laughed. Jennifer sat back down and smiled.

"Well that's good then. At least you've made a living for yourself. It must be nice to have a bit of money to spare." Her smile dropped as she had a light bulb moment. "The money in my account – that was you, wasn't it?"

"Yes."

"But...why? Why did you do that?"

"I needed to make sure she was safe. That you were all safe." He glanced over to the pushchair and back to Jennifer.

"How did you get my account details?"

"That was some old fashioned trash-digging I'm afraid." He laughed.

"I was so cruel to you, I –" she didn't look at him.

"It's in the past now, Jen. It's going to be okay." His deep voice was authoritative, but calm.

"But –"

"Enough, seriously. I forgive you." He stroked Katherine's hair and she stirred a little, but not enough to wake herself up.

"You never gave up, did you?"

"I made myself a rich man for a reason, Jen. I knew she was still alive and I needed to find her."

"But how?"

"Because people are worth a lot more than we give them credit for. Any other kidnapper would have asked for a ransom. She was out clubbing, which meant she was with someone –someone that would miss her. If people miss you enough, they will pay as much as it takes to get you back. But Marcus just took her, which made me wonder why. Then, when you told me about him and how you met and I saw how close you had got to him in such a short space of time, I knew something was up." Joe shifted a little, in order to reach his briefcase. He balanced it on the arm of the sofa and opened it. Inside, Jennifer could see numerous pieces of paperwork, but Joe pulled out a black binder, full of paperwork. He opened the binder and flicked a few pages until he found the right one. Joe handed Jennifer the binder. On the page was an image of Marcus, held in place onto a birth certificate by a paper clip.

"Who is Jack Turner?"

"Jack Turner is Marcus' real name." Joe reached over and flipped the page again. "This is the real Marcus." Jennifer stared at the document in front of her – a death certificate. "Marcus was a twelve year old boy who Turner killed in 1992. They were best friends at school. His death sent Turner crazy and he was institutionalised a year later. By the time he was released when he was 20, he had managed to convince the doctors he was sane. But then he disappeared, because there is no mention of Jack Turner after 2000."

"So, how did you know it was him?"

"Because I did some digging into your background: I'm sorry, but you were a suspect in my mind for a while."

Jennifer held back her anger. "What did you find?"

"You went to school with Jack Turner. And according to your old school records, he repeatedly beat you at school."

"I don't remember him; I don't even remember being bullied as a kid."

"Sometimes our brains block out unpleasant memories, which is why you never remembered it." Joe put the briefcase on the floor and took the binder back from Jennifer. He flicked to the back of the folder and handed it back.

"This," he said pointing to the document, "is a photo of him at school." She looked at the image: a class photograph. Joe's finger hovered over the image of a little boy with blonde hair, staring to his left.

"It looks nothing like Marcus, I mean Jack." Her glance shifted to the left following the boy's gaze and she saw her eleven-year-old self, with her hair in bunches. "That's me." Her shock rang out in her voice.

"You were in the same class, as you can see, he knew who you were, even back then."

"I don't understand: why did he come after me?"

"Who knows? Maybe in his twisted head, he thought he could pick up from where he left off. He was clearly obsessed with you."

"But he got confused and took Katherine?"

"It was dark in the club; he must have panicked and just assumed it was you."

"But he didn't tell Katherine any of this? She said he spoke to her about me all the time."

"He couldn't admit to himself that he wasn't Marcus, so why would he tell her?" Joe's voice was defensive, but ultimately still calm.

"I... I can't believe it. All this has happened because a boy from school had a crush on me? I can't even remember him!"

"Well, now you might – now you've seen his picture." Joe looked down at Katherine with love in his eyes. "I'm going to take her upstairs, put her to bed. Then we can talk about this a little more." Joe scooped the sleeping Katherine up into his arms and carried her out of the room. Jennifer was left alone in the living room, staring at her baby. She slid off of the sofa and crawled over to the pushchair. She picked the baby up, who was still fast asleep and cradled her. Tears poured from her eyes and her whole body shook.

"This is my fault, darling. I did this to us. I don't even remember him – how did I forget a whole person? Especially someone who hurt me? And my parents never said anything about me being bullied... did they even know?" She started to rock the baby from side to side, staring at her pink sleeping face and wishing she was a child again. *Maybe if I was a baby, I'd be happier*, she thought. Jennifer could hear Joe's footsteps coming from the room above her. *He seems so different from before, he used to be so... care-free. Katherine and Joe were just perfect, I thought they were going to get married, but then... then it all went wrong and now I barely recognise either of them.* She wiped a tear away from her eye as she heard Joe's heavy footsteps descend the stairs.

"You okay?"

"Yeah." She sniffed. "I was just checking on Little Katherine." Joe looked confused and then nodded as he mentally reminded himself of the baby's name. Jennifer stood up and walked out of the living room. "Tea?" she asked, her head in the fridge. "I'm kind of hungry."

"I'm not surprised; you haven't eaten since you got here."

"Old habits die hard, I'm afraid. It's all this eating rabbit food – it's thrown my appetite right off."

"I didn't want to say anything," he replied sarcastically, "but you are looking kind of chubby." He nudged her with his elbow and started rummaging through the cupboards for mugs and snacks.

"Am I?" Jennifer looked down and prodded her own stomach. "Maybe I've put on a couple of pounds. I didn't even notice…" her voice trailed off.

"I was only joking." He turned his attention to Jennifer and absent-mindedly ate the Jaffa Cakes he'd just found. "Anyway, I thought you said something earlier about you've been going to the gym a lot, you know – for the stress?"

"I have." Jennifer stepped back and tried to find a surface to lean against.

"So you can't have put weight on surely." He looked up. "What's wrong? You've gone a bit pale." Joe guided her to a wooden dining chair and fetched a glass of water. She burst into tears. "What? Jen, what's wrong?"

"I'm not fat."

"I didn't say you were." Joe looked concerned as he rubbed her back.

"No, I'm not fat." She looked angry, tears running down her face and fear in her eyes.

"Jen –." Joe knelt down on the floor next to her, looking up at her tear-streaked face helplessly.

"I'm pregnant." She took a sip of the water and then gently placed the glass on the oak dining table beside her. She wiped a water droplet from the side of the glass.

"Are you sure?"

"I've been losing weight for months and then suddenly I don't notice I've put on weight? It must be pregnancy."

"It could be all the stress and the take-out food –."

"No, I'm definitely pregnant." Jennifer sounded exhausted.

"Well how do you know?"

"Because I completely went off food when I was pregnant with Katherine, but kept putting weight on. They had to alter my wedding dress." She rubbed her temples.

Joe stood up abruptly, "Come on." He held out his hand.

"Where are we going?" he lead her out of the kitchen.

"The supermarket." Joe handed her a coat and then bounded upstairs. Jennifer heard him knock on a door and start talking. He then ran back downstairs and pulled Jennifer out of the house and to his car.

"Hey – stop!" She grounded her feet. "Why are we going to the supermarket?"

"Pregnancy test." He pressed a button on his key fob and the car unlocked.

"Well, who's going to watch the baby?" Jennifer shrugged the coat on and stepped forward a little.

"Kat's parents, don't worry she'll be fine." Joe opened the car door for her and the light came on.

"I – I don't want to know," she stuttered, looking at the concrete drive beneath her feet.

Joe slammed the car door shut. "Why not? Because the sooner you know, the sooner you can make some decisions."

"Decisions?" she glared at him.

"You know… decisions, about the pregnancy." Joe couldn't look at her for a moment.

"I'm not having an abortion."

"You say that now, Jen, but you may change your mind." Joe opened the car door.

"No, I won't." Jennifer pushed the car door shut, wrenching the handle out of his grip.

"Look, I don't like the idea either, a life is a life, but come on – do you really want to keep it knowing it's his?"

"That's like asking me to give Katherine away just because Marcus, I mean Jack–whatever, is her father."

"You didn't know then, about him." Joe looked her in the eyes.

"No…" Jennifer mumbled and her anger momentarily lapsed.

"But now you do and this time things are different." He dropped his gaze to his shiny leather shoes.

I can't do this… It's a child not a thing, she thought.

"I can't give it up," her voice cracked slightly.

"He kidnapped your best friend, all because he had a crush on you in school! He's dangerous. You can't keep this baby." The anger swelled in his voice.

"Why? Because it might turn into a murderous raving lunatic like its father?" She raised her voice and placed her palm flat onto her stomach.

"Yes."

"So Katherine is going to do the same is she?" She continued to yell at the man who had spent years trying to help her.

"Well –." He stammered.

"Well nothing – they are my children and I won't give them up without a fight. So, you are going to drop the idea of killing my unborn child and drive me to the supermarket, or you can go inside and forget about ever seeing Kat again." She opened the car door and Joe walked around, opening the driver's side. He stepped up into the car and sat down, starting the engine without a word. Jennifer climbed in and crossed her arms against her stomach. *I can keep it, can't I?* she cried to herself. Joe focused on reversing out of the drive.

When they arrived at the supermarket, the car park was nearly empty and they could see the late night shoppers milling around inside the brightly-lit shop which was as long as the car park was wide. They climbed out of the car and walked towards the supermarket in silence. It wasn't a cold night but Jennifer couldn't help but shiver. She felt sick to her stomach and her head pounded, making her dizzy. She leaned on Joe for support despite her better judgement. He took her by the arm and guided her to the automatic doors without a word.

When they were inside, Joe dragged her towards the health and beauty section and picked out a trustworthy looking pregnancy test. He pulled her over to the till, her eyes barely open and paid for the test. Joe escorted her out, ignoring the judgemental looks they were getting from fellow shoppers and put her back in the car. Jennifer closed her eyes for a second and the next thing she knew, she was on the sofa in Katherine's parents house. She felt a chill and looked out of the window: sunrise. Brushing the hair from her face, she sat up a little and saw Joe on the armchair across from her, his head propped up by a muscular arm as he tried to sleep.

Jennifer got up from the sofa and padded to the kitchen, realising she wasn't wearing any shoes. She smiled and shook away her shiver, looking for the mugs. She opened the cupboard and took a mug down, placing it quietly on the side. She heard movement in the living room and took another mug out of the cupboard. Jennifer started making tea, but she didn't have to turn around to know someone else was now in the room.

"Morning," said Joe's gruff voice as he tried to cough away the sleepiness. She waved at him over her shoulder, without turning and poured the steaming water into the two mugs, being careful not to spill any on her hands. Joe placed the milk carton next to her and she mumbled a thanks. When she finally turned around Joe was leaning against the wall with his eyes closed. Jennifer nudged him awake and handed him his tea.

"You and tea. You know there is more caffeine in coffee, right?" he grinned and winced as the tea burnt his lips. "When did you wake up?"

"A couple of minutes ago. What time is it?"

"About six, I think. Everyone else is still asleep."

"Oh, I need to check on Katherine and Kat." She looked confused and then laughed at her own sentence. "I really didn't think that name through, did I?"

"Well I doubt you expected all this to happen." He smiled but then a daunted look swept across his face and he stared into his tea.

"I'll go check on them." She put her tea down and walked out of the kitchen and through the living room to the stairs. She could hear the child giggling faintly and she walked faster. When she walked into the bedroom, Katherine was sat on the bed with the baby in her arms, pulling faces at her and making her laugh. She looked beautiful, the fresh dawn light shining through a gap in the curtains. Jennifer watched the dust in the air, curling around the room from the imaginary breeze. Her best friend was happy and alive, her daughter was growing into an amazing person and they were all about to start a new life together. She drank in the scene, leaning against the door frame, the oak door opened out into the room. Katherine looked up at Jennifer and smiled; she stood up with the child still in her arms and ran over to Jennifer. She embraced her, holding her tight and kissed her on the cheek.

"Thank you," she whispered. "Thank you so much."

"For what?"

"Just for being you, Jen. You didn't give up on me."

"But –"

"You named your daughter after me. It wasn't in memory of my death. It was in hope that I would come back." She beamed at her, brushing a strand of Jennifer's hair away from her face. "Thank you." They hugged again and then Jennifer managed to get hold of the baby so she could get her some breakfast. "Can I feed her? She makes the funniest faces."

"Uh, yeah – sure. Let's go downstairs though so we don't wake up your parents."

"Oh, good idea! I'll just get dressed and I'll meet you down there." Katherine walked back over to the bed and rummaged through the clothes Joe had got her, holding a dress up against her. Jennifer remembered when she went into labour with Katherine, how she had been wishing her pregnancy away, how she didn't want a baby. Now, she looked down at her giggling daughter and felt ashamed of her own actions. But despite the horror they had all been through, Katherine was healthy and growing. Jennifer sighed and walked out of the room, leaving Katherine to get changed.

Chapter Twenty One

Whilst Katherine fed the happy baby and Joe watched in awe with the clear look of paternal longing on his face, Jennifer snuck away upstairs with the pregnancy test Joe had bought her. He slipped it into her hand, as she walked past him, which went unnoticed by the pre-occupied Katherine who pulled faces at the messy infant. She went into the pristine white and duck-egg blue bathroom and locked the door behind her. Taking a breath, she opened the box and studied the instructions. It wasn't the first time she had taken a pregnancy test, but she was so nervous that reading the tiny font was the only thing that calmed her down, despite it's blurriness. She took the test and impatiently waited the three minutes for it to develop, tapping her foot on the white, shining floor tiles. She re-read the instructions just to be sure. She checked her watch and the time was up. She picked the test up and held it between her fingers, staring at the pink stripes: positive.

"Oh god," she sighed and bit her lip but was startled by a knock at the door.

"Everything alright in there?" The voice of Katherine's mother echoed in the hallway.

"Fine, yes, sorry." Jennifer wrapped the stick in tissue and thrust it to the bottom of the small wicker bin. She rinsed her hands and unlocked the door. "Sorry, bathroom's all yours." She plastered a fake smile on her face and edged around the elderly woman and raced down the stairs. Joe looked up at her with questioning eyes. She nodded and sat down on the sofa, staring at her best friend and her baby. Jennifer sat up straight, up her hands on her knees just staring. After a moment Joe had to cough at her to gain her attention, because Little Katherine was walking over to her. She smiled and welcomed her child into her arms.

"Come here you!" she put on a motherly tone and cuddled her child. "I love you. Do you love mummy?"

"Mummy! Mummy mummy... mummy!" The child mumbled her first word. Jennifer choked back the tears and looked at Joe and Katherine.

"Did she just–?" Joe gasped, pointing at the toddler and staring at Jennifer.

"Yes, it was definitely 'Mummy'." They smiled at the pair of them and Jennifer realised what she had to do. "I'm keeping it, Joe." She didn't look up to see his or Katherine's reactions, she just fussed over her little girl as she felt her heart ache with warmth.

****

The three adults, newly adorned with a sense of pride and hope, decided that at the end of the week they would have to look for somewhere to live. They had already agreed that Jennifer and the children would need their own place and Joe was insisting he pay for it despite her protests. Joe was a wealthy man now and he wasn't afraid to spend money where it was needed. Katherine wanted to stay with Jennifer, but she knew her place was by Joe's side. The relationship struggled to be what it was before: Katherine wasn't the same fun-loving care-free person . She was constantly looking over her shoulder. Joe and Jennifer did what they could to calm her, but some days were better than others. By the time they moved into their new house (Joe needing somewhere local to live for when he started the new branch of his business) Katherine was getting back to her old ways and Jennifer became PR Manager for Joe's UK branch of the company. The months whizzed by as the women settled into their intense but wonderful new lives. Jennifer often caught herself thinking it was all a dream, from which she would soon awake and find herself Marcus' prisoner - jut as Katherine had been. It took a long time for them to get over the shock of the situation, and they joked frequently at how money couldn't fix everything. But with time, and success came some form of consistent peace for the three of them.

When Jennifer was sixth months pregnant, Marcus was sent to prison for life and she decided it was time to say goodbye to the horrible ordeal that was her marriage. She left Little Katherine at home with the nanny and drove her new Ford to the prison and asked for a visit. Jennifer took a deep breath as the guard scanned her for metal objects. He let her pass and pointed to a table in the visitor's centre. She sat down and waited for Marcus to appear. Two minutes later, she was about to walk out when she saw a man with grey streaks in his hair and pain in his eyes walk into the room. He headed straight for her table and sat down wearily, supporting his weight as he sat by pushing his palms down onto the table.

"Hi." He coughed.

"Hello, Marcus – uh Jack, sorry." She couldn't look him in the eyes, so instead she looked at her black knee-length skirt. She loved her new job and everything about it (despite it's vastness and the sheer amount of responsibility she had), especially all the beautiful clothes she got to wear, but maternity work skirts were hard to come by in the designer ranges, so she had to settle for M&S. She made a mental note to start a maternity clothing range and then returned her attention to the man in front of her.

"Can I have a hug?"

"Um, okay." She stood up and hugged her stalker ex-husband, her pregnant belly a cause for confusion under her blouse. "Listen –." He stopped her words with a hand to her mouth.

"You're pregnant," he stated, glaring at her stomach as it was the first time he had noticed her bulging belly.

"Yes." she didn't smile as she usually would when someone asked about her unborn child. Instead, her face was cold and plain, the same way it looked when she spoke to clients who were hiding things from her. She'd been told many times that it was a nerving look and it had cracked many a devious man.

"Well, is it mine?"

"Of course it's yours." She sighed, looking at her manicured nails and touching the tips of them as she fiddled. Her new look was almost a pregnant-boss-lady-chic with a little bit of bitch thrown in. Jennifer didn't want to find herself in intimidating situations such as this one, so she dressed like a professional and shielded her heart from the world in many ways. But today, her shield was damaged and even her expensive clothes and freshly styled hair didn't seem to protect her from her ex-husband and her greatest fear.

"Boy or a girl?"

"Boy." She saw the pride in his eyes and it broke her heart – for a moment. She shrugged the emotions away and pretended to stifle a yawn.

"Is he okay?"

"He's fine. But he is the reason I am here." She placed her palms flat on her bump. "Marcus– sorry, Jack –." She corrected.

"Don't call me that. Why do they keep calling me Jack?" Jack looked pale and confused; his voice was weak in his throat.

"Because that's your name, Jack, remember?" She watched the light die from his eyes.

"I remember: I was just hoping it was a dream."

"It was more like a nightmare for me and Katherine. You kidnapped my best friend because you thought it was me and then you married me to fulfil some sick fantasy you had when we were kids. I don't even remember you!" she yelled, her rapid-fire words barely escaping her painted lips. The guard looked up at her, but she faked a smile and he looked back down.

"I remember you. I remember the first time I set eyes on you – we were in a coffee shop and you were reading." he smiled, but it only made Jennifer feel sick.

"No, Jack – we went to school together. You were sectioned for killing your best friend and then you stole his identity just so you could meet me again. Do you understand that that's wrong?" Jennifer started to think back to their relationship, trying to remember if he had been this insane when they were married. Then she realised that they were married because of his delusions and dismissed the vaguely happy memories of their time together and focused on all the pain the man in front of her had caused not just her, but her loved ones. He had destroyed so many lives to achieve a fantasy of love.

"Yes, but-," he stammered.

"But nothing: you are a criminal, a murderer, a liar, a kidnapper and a fraud. But do you know what?"

"What?" A hope lit his eyes.

"I loved you. I loved Marcus. You created the ideal man, you looked after me, you married me and you gave me two children." She cried, wiping a tear away from her eye.

"See – we're going to be okay. When I get out we can be a family." He reached out to hold her hand, but she snatched it away.

"No, Jack. After today, you are never going to see me or my children again. You're going to die of old age in here because you're insane and they would never let you leave – I'll make sure of it," she whispered angrily at him, her voice cracking under the pressure of her tears.

"I don't understand," he whined.

"You took my best friend and pretended to be someone you had killed! You ruined her life, her family's lives. You yanked me out of mine and made me a doting wife who hated herself. You ruined everything and I will never forgive you!" She stood, screaming at him – the whole room watching. She stepped sidewards and leaned down so she could reach him and whisper in his ear.

"The only thing keeping you alive right now is the fact that I don't want to give birth to my son in prison. Know this Marcus - if you ever manage to get out of here and you come looking for me or my children, I will kill you." She straightened up again and waved over the guard. The guard called on his radio and two more guards entered the room and approached the table.

"Everything alright, Miss?"

"No – take him away. I'm the last visitor he'll ever get." She screamed at Jack again, "I hope you rot in hell! You're a pathetic waste of space!" A guard tried to restrain her as she took a swing for Jack but it was too late. She punched his face, catching his nose and blood poured out of it. He sunk to his knees and Jennifer started kicking him, tears streaming down her face. "You ruined my life. I hate you!" The guards picked Jack up and pulled him out of her range. "You will never see my children! They will never know who you are!" The guards escorted him from the visitor's centre and the other guard restrained her and took her into the office. He handed her a tissue and she sank onto an office chair. He left her there for a moment and then returned with a cup of tea.

"He's a mess, you know. And he deserves it." He patted her roughly on the shoulder and left her alone to drink the sweet tea whilst he phoned Joe. A little while later he came back into the room and escorted her out of the building. Joe and Katherine were outside waiting for her and Joe took Jennifer's car home, whilst Katherine drove Jennifer.

"What happened?" Katherine asked once they had set off.

"I snapped, I just snapped." Jennifer stared at the main road ahead.

"You're lucky they didn't arrest you. Joe and I had to leave a board meeting for this, Jen." Katherine had joined Joe in the top ranks of the company and was on the board of directors, Joe was CEO and all three of them owned shares. Katherine clicked the indicator up and turned the corner. "You're not okay, are you?" she sighed.

"He took you!" Jennifer yelled, her hands animating her speech as she grew angry again.

"I know." She clicked the indicator down.

"He stole you from my life and then married me!"

"I know."

"He ruined everything," she mumbled under her breath, fiddling with a loose thread at the bottom of her blouse. She made a note to herself to complain to her fashion co-ordinator.

"I know, Jen! I know – I was there! He had me locked in a room for four years. Believe me; I know what that man is capable of. You had every right to go off on one, but it doesn't matter any more – he's locked up and you'll never see him again," she shouted, her eyes on the road.

"I told him I to rot in hell and that I hoped he died in prison."

"Good. I wish he was dead." She didn't look at Jennifer but she could feel her eyes burning into her. "I threatened to kill him."

"Jennifer, we are important people in an ever-expanding company: you can't just scream at people ."

"What do you expect me to do instead?"

"Calmly threaten them and walk out like a pro." She grinned and they both laughed.

Chapter Twenty Two

"Everything seems fine, Miss Hampton. How are you coping?" Dr Simmons, the company doctor, pulled the ultrasound screen away and cleaned up her stomach. She was having a check-up with the company medical team. Jennifer always proffered using the staff clinics to the public ones because they weren't allowed to ask her any personal questions - a perk of being a head of a multi-company conglomerate.

"I feel incredible, Doctor - both personally and professionally." She beamed up at him and her face glowed.

"Good." The doctor looked down at her chart. "It says in your file that you had a little trouble with your daughter's birth. Have you experienced any of the same symptoms this time around?"

"Not at all, I've been really happy, looking after myself, taking the right prenatal vitamins: all good." She pulled down her blouse and sat up, pushing her hands down on the bed for support. Eight months into her pregnancy and everyone was healthy, she couldn't ask for better news.

"Good and how is your daughter coping with the adjustments?" he scribbled notes down on his chart.

"Amazingly – she loves the new house and she understands that Mummy is having another baby, but that I still love her. She's a very well-adjusted child. We had a birthday party for her last week: she's three now. I've never seen a child so confused by presents in all my life!" Jennifer laughed but it was just to cover up her embarrassment at the questions he was asking. She shot him a warning look that he ignored.

"Well, I'm glad everything's going well for you. Oh and HR have asked me to remind you that you will need to have another medical examinations six months after the baby is born. Did you want me to schedule that in now?"

"Yes – but could you run it past my assistant, James – honestly I don't know how I lived without him!" She shrugged her blazer back on and picked up her black handbag from the chair at the end of the bed.

"Of course, Miss Hampton – do you have any questions at all?" He smiled a fake doctor smile and opened the door for her.

"No, not that I can think of." She smiled and went to exit the room.

"I must say, it is remarkable how you've adapted in such short a time." He pushed his luck.

"What do you mean?" She glared at him and stopped in her tracks, slamming the door shut.

"Well, you left a difficult family situation and ended up the Head of PR for a multi-national company. And now you're less than a month away from having your second child. It's very impressive." Jennifer winced as he spoke and her happy maternal instincts left her as she took on her business persona. "I'm sorry, Miss Hampton - I know we aren't supposed to bring it up…"

"No you aren't – it's company policy in fact. And, as my doctor you are privy to a lot more detail than the rest of the staff. I hope you aren't the gossiping type." Her clipped, authoritative voice sounded like a stranger speaking. Jennifer often wondered what had happened to her: when did she go from a confused house-wife to a corporate machine in high heels? She brushed the thought aside and continued on the defensive.

"No, ma'am." He swallowed and clutched the chart to his chest.

"Good, because if you were, you might find yourself in a lot of trouble. Good day Dr. Simmons." She flashed him a smile and marched out of the room, her high heels clicking on the tiled floor and left the doctor alone in the medical room fearing for his job. Jennifer got into the lift and pressed the down button. The soft lift music irritated her and she pulled out her dicta-phone, pushing the red button. "Note to staff: the discussion of the personal lives of the company bosses is a Code Red violation of your contracts and will lead to an enquiry as to your position with the company." She pushed the button again and put the dicta-phone back in her handbag. The lift doors opened and she stepped out onto the 9th floor, into the corridor that led to her office. Either side of the corridor were twelve smaller offices: six on either side. These belonged to PR staff and the one directly next to her office on the left, belonged to her assistant, James. As Jennifer walked along the corridor, various office doors opened and people emerged with memos and documents for her attention. James rushed to her side, a hands-free ear piece in his left ear and a takeaway cup in his right hand. She regularly compared it to her tiny book-store, which she had long since purchased and improved, whilst holding on to it's rustic charm.

"Miss Hampton, here's some water. I thought you might be thirsty." He handed her the cup.

"Thank you, James." She sipped as she walked, people dutifully following her up the long corridor until she dismissed them into their offices, barking orders at them. "Marge – get Carter from HR in my office, ASAP. Luke, I need to cancel my six o'clock hair appointment: the nanny wants to talk to me. Rachel, find me a new nanny that knows how to tell the time. Sarah, grab me a tea would you? And bring me the 7'14 merger documents; I want to review their contracts." She finished her water and James took the cup from her.

"Miss Hampton, I've got Katherine and Joseph on line two, Dr. Simmons on line three and your daughter on line four." James spoke fast in order to keep her attention. He was the only one that didn't fear for his job, but he still had enough sense not to abuse his position.

Jennifer stopped, "Why have you got my daughter on line four?" she ran/wobbled to her office, holding her stomach to support it and opened the door. She sat down on her large black leather desk chair, picked up the phone and hit line four. "Darling what's the matter?" Little Katherine mumbled something about wanting a new dress and the nanny wouldn't take her. "Sweetie, Mummy's at work right now." The child mumbled again in her half-speech-half-gibberish way that only Jennifer could seem to understand. "Okay, well what was the dress you wanted? The red one with the bows?" Jennifer looked at the time on the phone. "Well, I'll tell you what, why don't I come and pick you up and we can go and have lunch together and then buy you the dress?" Little Katherine squealed. "Okay darling, put the nanny on the phone. Helen? Yes, it's me – I'll be there in about half an hour to pick her up. Okay, bye." She hung up the phone and hit line two. "Hey guys, what's up – how's Italy?" She crossed her legs over as she asked, glancing down at her swollen feet.

"Oh you would love it, Jen! It's so sunny and there's hot Italians everywhere." Joe's deep voice echoed through the phone. "Not why we're calling though – how did the check-up go? Is the rock star baby doing okay?"

"The baby's fine, thanks. That doctor on the other hand..." she muttered, the annoyance obvious in her tone.

"What did he do?" Joe asked, almost mocking her - but in a nice way. Jennifer had earned a reputation for being easily annoyed by the staff: there was a problem almost every week. Luckily, she only had the rights to dismiss her own people and not those from the other areas of the company. That privilege belonged to Joe and Katherine alone.

"Mentioned things way above his pay grade."

"Fire him then?"

"He meant it in good faith; I'll just scare him a little, that should do the trick. I need to go and pick up Katherine for some dress shopping – you two have fun!" She hung up the phone again. Clicking onto line three, she politely told Dr. Simmons that she couldn't speak to him right now and then hung up but that he should expect a phone call from someone in the next few days. *That should keep him on his toes,* she thought. She clicked the intercom button, "James, get in here." Her voice was starting to tire at this point.

James opened the door and stepped quietly into the room. "Yes, Miss Hampton?"

"Cancel my day – I'm taking Katherine shopping." She came out from behind her desk, tidying paperwork as she half-circled the desk.

"What about the merger documents?" He bit his lip as he questioned his boss. She could see the look of regret on his face, but it quickly faded when she didn't yell at him or cry.

She considered the question for a second, "I'll take them home with me. Where's Sarah with my tea?" When James didn't answer she walked out of the office to find Sarah curled up in her own office desk chair with tears pouring down her eyes. "Sarah? What's wrong?"

"Oh, I am so sorry Miss Hampton; I will go and get that tea you asked for." She made a move to stand, but Jennifer stopped her.

"Hush now and forget the bloody tea. What's the matter, dear?" Jennifer perched on the edge of Sarah's desk, well aware there were fifteen pairs of eyes staring through the office divider windows but it was too late - her maternal instincts had kicked in.

"I'm pregnant." The girl wailed.

"That's wonderful news, Sarah – why are you crying?" she asked, deciding whether to embrace the girl or not.

"My husband left me when he found out. He doesn't want children." Sarah drew her knees to her chest, her skirt riding up a few inches but not enough to expose anything other than her thigh. Her long blonde hair covered her shaking shoulders.

"Well then, sweetie, you don't want him." she said - her expression was plain, but grinning internally.

"What?" Sarah looked up in wonder, shocked, at her usually terrifying boss.

"Men: who needs them? Work and our children are the important things in life." Jennifer smiled. "That, and designer wardrobes."

"Yes, b-but I can't..." she stuttered through the tears.

"Can't what?"

"I can't afford a baby by myself, how am I going to raise a child when I'm constantly working?"

"We can fix that."

"Oh no, please don't fire me, Miss Hampton!" Fear swept across her face.

"Why on earth would I fire you?" She sighed, "How long have you been with the company, Sarah?"

"From day one, Miss Hampton. I was one of the first people Mr. Joe hired for your team." The girl hiccuped.

"So I have no need to fire you, if Joe thinks you're worth it – then so do I. He certainly wouldn't have appointed you to my division if he didn't trust you." She stood up and straightened her skirt. "No, I think a raise is in order, Sarah. How does an extra £10K sound?"

"That sounds amazing, Miss Hampton, thank you so much!" the woman sobbed gently.

"I tell you what, I'll throw in a nanny as well, I'm getting a bit bored of her anyway – all paid for." Jennifer tried to sound casual with her generosity in order to stop the other staff expecting handouts. But everyone already knew that pregnant or abused women were a chink in her armour.

"Miss Hampton, I don't know what to say." Sarah stood up and hugged her, then she let go as if she had just hugged a grizzly bear. Jennifer smiled down at her and winked as if it was their little secret that she wasn't a corporate bitch all the time.

"Say nothing and go home, have the day off: paid leave. Don't worry about a thing. Tell James what you were supposed to do today and he will cover it." Jennifer stood back, patted the girl on the arm and walked out of the office. As she did so, the staff stood in awe as she entered the lift for the second time in twenty minutes. "Make good choices, kids," she called and winked as the doors shut in front of her. It was safe to say that Jennifer certainly confused her staff. But they liked her, even though she went from mother to monster in sixty seconds. She was a good boss and a loyal one at that. No one waved back, but instead carried on with their work days - some of them huddling around Sarah as she started to cry with joy, telling the others how the conversation had gone with the infamous Jennifer Hampton.

****

Jennifer held Little Katherine's hand as she toddled through the shops looking at the pretty dresses. Today, she had decided to dress as Merida from Disney's *Brave*, so she wore a green medieval dress with long sleeves and a skirt that reached the floor. She had learned not to trip over it and instead gently kicked the dress forward so as not to step on the hem. Jennifer had learned not to stifle her daughter's strong personality a long time ago, so the little girl picked intriguing outfits to wear for her little outings into the world. It only made Jennifer chuckle as she observed her toddler acting like a confused princess. The child pointed at various dresses in the store, in a motion she wanted them, but she knew the golden rule: she had to ask nicely if she hoped to get anything. If Jennifer had done anything right it was to make sure she didn't raise a brattish child. Finally, after much searching, the little girl gestured to a scarlet prom-style netted dress with a black bow around the middle.

"Mummy, please?" she pointed again.

"Please what, Katherine?" She asked the toddler.

"Please this dress, Mummy?" She gave her the cutest smile she could and Jennifer caved. She grinned, found the right size on the rack and then she knelt on the floor in front of her daughter and held the dress up to her small body.

"You like this one, then?"

"Yes, Mummy!" the girl exclaimed.

"Okay darling, well it's only £30, would you like to pick another dress, or get things to match this one?"

"Dress, please, thank you, Mummy. I love you!" She hugged Jennifer.

"I love you too, sweetie." She stood up and took her daughter's hand again. "Now, let's go find another dress, shall we?" But, as she started to walk, she felt a crippling pain in her stomach. When she tried to ignore it, the pain got worse. "Actually hunny, can we look for the dress tomorrow? Mummy doesn't feel very well." The child nodded and they approached the counter. As they cued, the pain worsened and by the time they reached the check-out, Jennifer was doubled over with pain.

"Miss, are you alright?"

"No, I think the baby's coming." Jennifer sat down on the floor, sweat pouring down her face and she stared at her daughter, who looked terrified.

"Call an ambulance!" somebody yelled. Jennifer pulled her phone out of her handbag.

"James, meet me at the hospital and take Katherine home. I'm going into labour." She hung up the phone and closed her eyes.

Chapter Twenty Three

Jennifer opened her eyes and saw Katherine and Joe sitting by her beside. She tried to talk but her throat was dry. Katherine handed her some water and she took it gratefully.

"What are you doing here? You're supposed to be on holiday."

"James called us and told us what happened." Jennifer looked down at her stomach and realised she no longer held her son within her body. "He's okay – don't panic. They did an emergency C-Section."

"Why?"

"You went into a coma." Katherine glanced sideways at Joe.

"I knew I should have fired that doctor." Jennifer said nothing and placed her hands on her now considerably empty tummy.

"They said you are both lucky to be alive. They had to put him in intensive care because he was quite small still."

"How much does he weigh?" She tried to sit up, but exhaustion got the better of her and she gave up.

"He was 5 lbs 5 ounces at birth and his lungs weren't fully developed yet."

"Was?" Jennifer looked at her best friends with fear in their eyes. "How long was I out?"

"Six weeks."

"I – I've missed six weeks? Well is he okay now? Can I see him? Where's Little Katherine?"

"Calm down, everything's been taken care of. The doctor said you need to relax because your body is still really weak."

"Well, how long until I can go home?"

"They want to keep you in for a few more days to do some tests, to see why you slipped into a coma in the first place, but then you are free to go home." Katherine grasped her hand tightly. "We were so worried about you, Jen. I'm so glad you're okay."

"I'm always okay." She smiled weakly.

"Now, are you up for some good news?"

"Of course!" She sat up, this time with Joe's help.

"Okay," Katherine smiled and looked at Joe, "we're having a baby!"

"Oh my god that's amazing – congratulations! When did you find out?" she exclaimed, leaning to hug them both.

"In Italy – I thought I had food poisoning, turns out it was morning sickness. I'm three months along." They separated from the embrace and sat there smiling to each other. "We're going to get married next month. So I was wondering if you would like to be my Maid of Honour?"

"Yes, I will!" The women giggled and hugged again.

"Okay, well we are going to go for now, so just rest up and do what the doctors tell you to."

"I will – can you tell the nurse I want to see my son?"

"Sure." The couple walked out holding each other's hands and smiling. Jennifer grinned after them and then looked down at her stomach. *I wonder what he looks like*, she thought, stroking her stomach.

Chapter Twenty Four

"Phillip darling, can you get the shopping out of the car? Oh and do you know where your sister is?" Jennifer asked as she climbed out of the driver's side clutching her designer purse.

"No, Mum. Do you want the bags in the kitchen?"

"Yes, but stay out of the maid's way – I can't keep apologising to her because you trip her up!" She smiled and locked the car door. She walked up to the house, her heels clicking on the concrete and through the open door. "Katherine?"

"Yeah?" A girly teen answered her, yelling from her top floor bedroom.

"Come down a minute would you?" she heard her sixteen-year-old race down three flights of stairs, nearly falling on the last step. "Slow down!" Jennifer called as she walked into the kitchen.

"What's up?" Katherine's jeans hung on her hip, letting a flash of skin show between the top of her bleached denim waistband and the bottom of her black vest top.

"Okay, so I know you wanted to ask me something about the prom, so what was it?"

"I was wondering if I was allowed to go to the party afterwards?"

"Are Lily and Merry going?"

"Yes," Katherine mumbled.

"Is your boyfriend going – and don't lie to me?" Jennifer pursed her lips, pretending to be cross with her daughter.

"Yes, Jake will be there," the girl mumbled again, her long blonde her falling over her right eye.

"No, you can't go." Jennifer waited for the teenager to freak out.

"But Mum that's so not fair!" Katherine flung her arms in the air and huffed.

"Sorry, you can't go – you're busy." She held back a grin.

"No, I cancelled my horse riding lessons the next day," the girl argued.

"I know, but you can't go because you, Jake, Lily and Merry are all going to Paris for a week." Jennifer grinned as her daughter screamed with joy in front of her, jumping up and down on the spot. Jennifer held the maid knock something over as the screaming startled her.

"Oh my god, Mum – thank you thank you thank you! You are so cool!" She hugged her mother tightly and then let go.

"Be ready in ten minutes."

"Why where are we going?" she enquired, breathless.

"Shopping of course! I can't send you off on holiday without some new clothes." She winked as her daughter squealed again, pulling out her mobile phone and running out of the room. She heard Katherine on the phone to Lily, asking did she know the whole time and chatting about what she should wear. Jennifer had had the holiday planned for weeks, so of course her friends knew. Phillip shuffled into the room carrying the last of the shopping and Jennifer beckoned him over. "Darling, come and give your old Mum a cuddle." She grabbed him and tousled his hair; he gave her a big bear hug in return. "You're a sweet boy, you know that?"

"I know, you say it all the time, Mum, and you're not old" he whined, jokingly.

"Yeah, but at least I mean it. How was school?" She let him go and started unpacking the shopping.

"Good, thanks. I got a B on my maths test!" he beamed with pride.

"That's great, kid – high five!" Jennifer high-fived her son but then noticed a look in his eyes. "What's wrong, sweetie – did something happen at school?"

"No, nothing like that, it's just that when I got home the land-line was ringing so I answered it."

"Yeah?" She sat down at the breakfast bar. "Who was it?" she fiddled with the grapes in the fruit bowl in front of her.

"It was a detective; he said to tell you to call back as soon as possible." Phillip looked confused.

"Did he say why?" Jennifer turned pale as her son relayed the information, unaware of what was happening. She had decided a long time ago that her children didn't need to know about their father, for their own sake. And for her own. Jennifer, Kat and Joe had all agreed that the children were best off not knowing the ghosts of the past: but it looks like the ghosts were about to comes back to haunt them.

"He said something about a guy called Jack. Does he work for you?" Phillip picked a grape from the bunch and bit it in half, but he stopped eating when he realised his mother looked like she was about to pass out right there in the kitchen.

"No, Jack doesn't work for me. I'll be back in a second babe; can you unpack the shopping for me? There's a good boy" She ruffled his hair absent-mindedly and abandoned the conversation. She didn't wait for a response, but instead walked out of the kitchen and right along the hallway to her office. She turned on the light in the small room and picked up the phone and dialled the precinct number from the phone book. She glanced at the photos of her children on the walls of the office as the phone rang. Jennifer tapped the side of the phone impatiently, her heart thumping in her chest as her mind races to all the possibilities, all the reasons Johnson would possibly have for wanting to speak to her.

"DI. Johnson, please – tell him it's Miss Hampton." She waited for a moment until she heard some rustling at the other end and she heard his voice. "What's happened?"

"I'm glad you got my message, Miss Hampton." He sounded as stressed as she felt, and it only made her feel worse.

"Yes, my son passed it on." She swallowed as the nerves got the better of her.

"Oh, I see. Well, as you know, Jack was up for parole this week."

"Yes, and?" Her impatience got the better of her for a second, but then she checked herself.

"He was denied it." Johnson stated.

"Oh?" Jennifer held her breath for a moment.

"Then he didn't show up for roll call. Miss Hampton, I'm so sorry, but he passed away at 11:56 this morning. I –"

"How?!" she screamed, interrupting him.

"He hung himself." Jennifer put down the receiver and sat in her office chair. A knock at the door a moment later startled her.

"Come in." Katherine and Philip gingerly opened the door and walked into the cramped office.

"Are you okay, Mum?"

"No, darlings, I am not okay." Jennifer didn't bother wiping the tears away.

"Did someone die?"

"Yes," she sobbed.

"Who was it?"

"Jack Turner, but I knew him as Marcus." The two teenagers looked at each other in confusion and then simultaneously hugged their crying mother.

"Who was he, Mum?" Philip asked, whispering a little as he held her with his slim teenage arms.

"He was your father."

Acknowledgements:

I'd like to say thank you to Lara for listening to me go on about this book(and for the copious amounts of tea). Thanks Debbie for her beautiful artwork. Thank you to Carol, Paul, Eliza, Faye and Lorna for reading over the original drafts. Thank you to Stewart and Lucy for reading over the some of the final drafts before my re-write.

Thanks to Heidi for taking the time to read over Searching For Katherine and helping me decide to wait. The book has progressed so much since that afternoon in Browns.

Thanks to all of my friends for supporting me. Thanks to Mark Baker-Gooderson for lending me his name - I told you I'd write a book with you in.

A special mention goes to Andy and Sue: you are the ones that I could rely on to support me in my endeavours, especially when I considered throwing in the towel. Thank you for that, you have no idea how much it means to me.

I'd also like to thank everyone who bought my first book. It may have only been a few pennies to you, but to me it was encouragement to carry on writing. And to all those that bought this one and read to the end. This book is my pride and joy - nothing has made me happier. Except maybe tea.

Made in the USA
Charleston, SC
22 October 2014